Leeza McAuliffe Has Loads More To Say

✳ ✳ ✳

Nicky Bond

TAKE-AWAY-TEA BOOKS

Copyright © 2024 by Nicky Bond.

All rights reserved. No part of this publication may be reproduced, distributed or transmitted in any form or by any means, including photocopying, recording, or other electronic or mechanical methods, without the prior written per-mission of the publisher, except in the case of brief quotations embodied in critical reviews and certain other noncommercial uses permitted by copyright law. For permission requests, write to the publisher, addressed "Attention: Permissions Coordinator," at the address below.

Nicky Bond/Take-Away-Tea Books
https://nickybond.com

Publisher's Note: This is a work of fiction. Names, characters, places, and incidents are a product of the author's imagination. Locales and public names are sometimes used for atmospheric purposes. Any resemblance to actual people, living or dead, or to businesses, companies, events, institutions, or locales is completely coincidental.

Book design © 2024 BookDesignTemplates.com

Cover design/Portal Design and Illustration

Leeza McAuliffe Has Loads More To Say/Nicky Bond — First Edition

ISBN 978-0-9956574-5-8

Contents

New Year, New You 1

Weirdness 27

Do Your Best, Applemere 51

More-Happy Than Not-Happy 78

Adults Need To Adult 104

Family Dramas – Plural 132

Wingspreading 160

Problem Solving On High 185

Real Talk 216

Grandma x 2 248

The Worst Of Times 273

Happy Families 300

Acknowledgements 339

For Edith

1

New Year, New You

<u>Sunday 1st January</u>

'My name's Leeza McAuliffe, I'm 11 years old, and my family does my head in.'

If I were writing a book, that's how I'd start. Straight to the point, no messing around. Like the opening of 'Catcher in the Rye' that Will lent me last year. It was tricky to read but I remember the start. 'If you want to know who I am, I'll tell you I guess.' Not those exact words, but something like that. Anyway, this is my diary so I'll tell YOU, I guess. I was born in Manchester, I moved to the countryside last year (AKA the middle of nowhere) and yesterday I STARTED MY PERIODS. Woohooo. It's all go.

Mum invited the neighbours for a New Year buffet. (Christmas party food, going cheap.) Jake, his mum, and his grandad turned up at 8. They live closest. It's still a ten-minute walk down the lane but that's the countryside for you. Luckily, Jake's my best mate. As he's the only other young person this side of the village, it's important to get on.

After tea we snuck off to watch Netflix. I was still feeling excited about everything. Yesterday was a big deal. I ummed and ahhed, but in the end I told him. About my periods. I knew it was TMI but it was still my news. He actually surprised me. 'That's cool, Leez. Congratulations!' I must've looked shocked. 'What's up with your face?' he said. I shook my head. 'I didn't think you'd congratulate me. I thought you'd say it was gross. Most boys would.' 'Duh,' he said. 'It's just science, innit. And as if I'm like most boys. No way.'

Jake's going to be 14 this year. He's so mature already. Later on, when we came downstairs, Cait (his mum) made a show of us. 'Remember that age, Molly?' she said to Mum. Wasn't it fun? BFFs and crushes and romance!' Mum smiled but we did not.

* 2 *

(I actually eye rolled. I'm good at an eye roll. Mum says one day I'll roll them so far back they get stuck. I know she's joking but knowing my luck, I probably will.)

Monday 2nd January

I'm easing into this year's diary. I don't want to overdo it. There's no point writing pages every night when I still have Christmas homework. Besides, I'm dealing with my new body changes. Mum asked me how I felt and I said OK. She thought I might have stomach ache. I don't but I do have butterflies. I suppose that's because of the period and because I'm becoming a grown-up woman. I say that but I still refuse to wear dresses and I'm happiest in my PJs. Not walking up and down like a fashion model. (I know men can be models too. Or anyone for that matter. I just don't want to be stared at all the time. Maybe I will when I'm older.)

Tuesday 3rd January

Hello Auction Bidders! Are you still there? I enjoyed thinking about you last year. If you're new to this, let me explain. No one will read this diary as long as I live. But one day, hundreds of years from now, it might get sold at an auction. Like a historical source! If it does, and you've bought it, let me say HELLO AUCTION BIDDERS! I'm here to explain the everyday life of an almost-teenager in the English countryside.

Today was rubbish. I'd left every piece of homework until the last minute. When will I learn? It's because this holiday was packed. With Christmas and Grandma and Will's wedding, I've not had a minute. We're seeing them in a few days before they go on honeymoon. It's nice to finally have a grandad.

<u>Wednesday 4th January</u>
Back to school.

Today didn't start well. I was on time but the bus was not. It pulled up outside Jake's mini supermarket, 15 minutes late. If I were Grandma, I'd have rung the bus company and kicked off before I'd arrived at school. But then Grandma has a phone and I don't. This is one of many ways my life isn't fair. When we arrived, we went straight into double Maths. Rubbish.

There's a new person in class. Poppy. Her family have moved to Applemere, on the estate past the pub. It's nice not being the new girl anymore. I'm part of the furniture now. At least that's how it'll look to Poppy.

Miss Wilkinson was pleased with anyone who handed in homework. She won't be pleased when she sees my crossings out and mistakes. Maths is not my strength.

Thursday 5<u>th</u> January

Now I'm wondering what *are* my strengths. I like English and History but I wouldn't say they're strengths. I like reading, I like watching films, and I like writing my diary. Maybe I'm a natural storyteller.

Friday 6<u>th</u> January

Judging by the comments on my English homework, I am NOT a natural story teller. It's Grandma's and Will's fault. Their wedding took up all my time. I'll have to look for my talents elsewhere.

I didn't tell them that. Grandma and Will, that is. (Keeping up, Auction Bidders?) They're staying tonight, on their way up to Scotland. 'We're having a low-key honeymoon, Molly,' was what Grandma said to Mum. But then she showed us pictures of their hotel. It was an actual castle! Mum did what she often does when Grandma talks. She snorted.

It was lovely to see photos of their wedding. I know I said I hate dresses but I made an exception for my bridesmaid's one. It looked great. Mum said she'd get a couple of pictures framed. She knows it's rare for the McAuliffe family to look presentable.

Saturday 7th January
Grandma said something funny yesterday. 'New Year, New You'. It was when Mum asked if her hair was lighter. She didn't say 'yes' or 'no'. Just 'New Year, New You'. Is this a thing? Do I need a new me? It's hard enough knowing who I was before. When your periods arrive on New Year's Eve, the year starts with a bang. (Btw, I was all done by Wednesday. I absolutely nailed it!)

Sunday 8th January
It was - and these were Mum's exact words - a cleaning and tidying day. (I should've realised when she tied her hair up in a high pony. She only does that when she's cleaning.) I pretended I had homework but Dad

saw me do it yesterday. There was no escape. As the oldest, I knew I had to set an example, but I also knew I didn't want to spend my Sunday sweeping up pine needles and taking down decorations. I kept calm. Spike did not. He deliberately knocked the dust pan out of my hand and kept storming off. Blane was no help either. He whined, on and off, all afternoon. (Classic Blane.) Kenny played with his blocks next to Harvest, who bounced in her bouncer. And clapped. She claps a lot atm. As usual it was left to me. I always have to be the sensible one.

Monday 9th January

I told Jake about Tidying Day on the bus. He said, 'Nightmare, Leez.' He was sympathetic but told me it's my own fault for having a big house. He was only joking but I still forget that we've got more space now. The house move feels like a blur. And we'd only been here a month before Harvest was born. There's no point buying a bigger house if you add extra people. And it's not as if we're rich. We bought an old wreck that no one wanted. It's still a bad idea when you look at it like that.

Jake lives with Cait and Tom. That's his mum and grandad, in case you Auction Bidders have forgotten. They live above the mini supermarket in the village. I like Jake's flat. It's warm and cosy. I always have a good time there. My house is draughty, smells of nappies, and there's always someone having a tantrum. Extra space doesn't matter when you're dealing with that.

We've a new class novel to read. 'The Diary of a Young Girl' by Anne Frank. It'll be interesting to compare her diary with mine over the weeks.

<u>Tuesday 10th January</u>
It's freezing. Literally. When I walked past the car this morning, it was covered in frost. At breakfast Dad said to Mum, 'Remember when we'd toss a coin to see who'd be scraping before work?' I think he used to rig it so he'd win. It was always Mum outside. She picked up Harvest in her bouncy chair and started to go upstairs. 'See you in the office, Mac', she said, as she left the room. With their new HR business from home, the car can stay frosty all day. And Harvest can bounce in the corner of the bedroom. I don't know what I want

to do when I'm older, but maybe starting a business from home is the way to go. If I can wear PJs all day, I'm in.

I've still not warmed up from the bus stop. Even Dad wasn't wearing shorts today. (Dad ALWAYS wears shorts.) It must be cold.

Wednesday 11th January

Spike was in a strop when I got in. With good reason this time. There's no point buying him seeds for Christmas, if he's not allowed to plant them. Obvs it's too frosty and they'll die, but I can see why he was annoyed. 'This is messed up,' he kept saying, every time Dad said no. (If he didn't have a buzz cut, he'd have torn his hair out, he was that mad.) In the end, he had to make do with the iPad, researching when to chit his potatoes. I've no idea what that means but it's what he researched.

I think Mum and Dad are doing 'New Year, New You' on Spike. He was never into gardening before but they're forcing him into a hobby. It's probably to calm him down. Stopping him eating sweets never worked so this is their next try. I still don't know what my 'New Year, New You' should be. What do I want to change? What was I like before?

Thursday 12th January

I pondered those questions all day. After school I put my Christmas presents on my bed to analyse. It might explain how people see me. There was my diary, some books, my new dressing gown, and my absolute favourite - marzipan fruits. (Only 2 left!) It's no help because I've been given a similar set of presents for the last few Christmases. Like no one thinks I've changed since I was 7! That's ridic because I was a kid then, and in 16 months I'll be a teenager. I should be offended.

The trouble is, I love writing this diary, I love getting new books, my dressing gown's really warm, and marzipan fruits taste amazing. But someone 16 months away from their teens shouldn't want the same things as when they were a kid. I'm confused.

Friday 13th January

I asked Mum. 'How do I seem to you?' I said. 'Fine,' she said. She was cooking so it wasn't the best time. I tried again. 'How do you think I act? What do you think I'm good at or interested in?' She didn't get it. 'You're good at all sorts of things and you can be interested in anything you want to be.' Then she ruffled my head (get off!) and finished measuring spices.

The spices were for Friday Fooday. Yes, it's back! Dad used his hands to blow a trumpet noise as we were getting up. 'Hear ye, hear ye, Friday Fooday will recommence this evening after its winter break!' He was being silly but we laughed anyway. Sometimes you need something to look forward to and Friday Fooday ALWAYS cheers me up.

In English we started talking about Anne Frank's diary. Ms. Phelps explained how Anne hid in a secret part of her house when the Nazis wanted to kill her family. It was shocking. I knew a bit about the war but not from a young girl's perspective. I thought it was only men, in black and white, fighting in the past. Sometimes I realise there's so much I still don't know. And I already know loads. How will everything fit in my head? I'll start reading the book tomorrow.

The good news is that after the build-up, Friday Fooday did NOT let me down. Mum and Dad had cooked vegetable laksa with homemade flat bread. It was delish. I'm always happy to eat food that's taken effort. Yesterday was cheese on toast. It was all right, but still.

Saturday 14<u>th</u> January
Reading for homework is the best. I started 'The Diary of a Young Girl' this morning and couldn't put it down. I've read well more than we were told to. Ms. Phelps won't mind. How can she be cross when I've done extra?

It's mad though. Even though Anne's from years ago, and even though she has to live in secret, she still writes about normal things. The first pages were about the children in her class. And she was funny! She wrote exactly what she thought of them and it wasn't always kind. She writes her diary for Kitty. Ms. Phelps told us that's her imaginary friend. Maybe I need my own Kitty to act as my pretend reader. I'll think about it before I go to sleep.

Sunday 15th January

Face palm! I already have a Kitty! It came to me when Kenny was hopping in front of the TV as we watched an old 'Horrible Histories'. Auction Bidders, YOU are my Kitty! Yes, the people who've paid money for my diary, years from now. How are you, out there in the future? I hope you're enjoying my life. To sum up, I still don't know who I am, who I want to be, and how I'm ever going to convince Mum and Dad that I need a phone. These are my current problems.

Monday 16th January

It's weird. I'm reading Anne Frank's diary just as the Auction Bidders are reading mine. Except my life isn't in danger. Apart from climate change. I know climate change is massive and needs sorting, but my day-to-day life is still better than Anne's. Even I can see that.

Tuesday 17th January

Grandma rang as we were finishing tea. I knew it was her because Mum kept saying 'Right' and 'Oh' while the other person didn't stop. That's defo Grandma. I can always tell. Her and Will are stopping here on their way back from their Scottish honeymoon. Mum said, 'The spare room might not be good enough if you're used to a swanky hotel.' Then Grandma said something else and Mum rolled her eyes, saying, 'Charming.' I know Grandma. She'll have been rude about our house. That's how she is.

When Mum hung up, Dad said, 'And how is the lovely Ursula?' (That's Grandma's name. FYI.) Mum harrumphed (I think that's the sound she made) and said, 'Exactly the same, Mac, exactly the same.'

Wednesday 18th January

Jake's a school year older than me but we're both in Class 1. That's what happens when your high school is teeny tiny with only 50 students. I'm used to it now. Sometimes I think about my old life and my old friends in Stockford High. There's nearly 2000 people there. That reminds me, I must message Jenna. I wonder if the weather's this cold in Manchester.

Last lesson was Art. Self-portraits. I thought I knew how to draw a picture of myself but apparently not. According to Mr Davies, eyes are exactly halfway down the face and the ears are right next to them, not at the side of the cheeks. I've been drawing everything in the wrong place for years.

I asked Jake if I'd drawn a good likeness of myself. He said, 'Pretty good.' Then I said, 'How do I seem when you look at me?' He stared for a sec and said, 'You seem completely random and ask stupid questions.' Then he smiled and went back to his portrait.

First Mum and now Jake. No one is helpful in my quest.

Thursday 19th January

This time last year I was massively stressed over Mum's birthday. It was her 40th and even though I had brilliant plans, I left them too late. (OMG that massive list! Remember? I had to write '40 Reasons Why You Are Nice.' It was SO hard to come up with 40.) This time it's easier. 41 is not as important. I don't need to try as much. Dad said he'd take us to the shops on Saturday and we can all choose something.

We hardly ever go shopping. The mini supermarket is where we get most of our food. Every so often we get a delivery from the Tesco on the retail park, (for big stuff like loo roll) and everything else is online. That's why Saturday will be a massive deal.

Friday 20th January
When I got in from school, Grandma and Will were on the sofa. Will was giving Harvest her bottle and she was wearing a bib that said 'Bonnie Wee Bairn' on it. I knew what that meant. Presents!

We all got a mug that said I LOVE SCOTLAND plus a big box of shortbread and a tartan blanket for the sofa. Over tea Grandma said, 'I tried to find something in McAuliffe tartan but apparently it's Irish. Did you know that, Sebastian?' Dad pulled a face at hearing his real name (everyone calls him Mac) and said, 'As far as I know I'm as Mancunian as they come.' Grandma said, 'I wonder if your parents would know?' and Dad shrugged. He hasn't spoken to his parents since he married Mum. They didn't approve, so I'm told. Not that I'm told much.

Apart from that awks moment, Friday Fooday was another triumph. At one point during tea, Grandma said, 'Don't you think it's time to stop this now?

Fooday. It highlights your sloppy elocution. FOOD DAY. That's how to say it.' Dad helped himself to the garlic potatoes and said, 'It's tradition, Ursh. A food-filled family meal every Friday. We can't change it now.' He smiled, knowing how annoyed she'd be. 'Don't call me Ursh,' she snapped. He put on a serious face and said, 'Sorry, that'll be my sloppy elocution.' Everyone giggled.

It's always funny when Dad and Grandma pretend to row. Then Spike said, 'We can't change fooday because it rhymes with pooday and every day is poo day here.' No one laughed (except Spike) although Mum said, 'You got that right,' as she sniffed Harvest's nappy and took her off to change. Grandma was still on one. She likes standards and manners - anything that feels uncomfortable and stiff. She said, 'Spike, that's far too unsavoury for the dinner table.' Will winked at me as he reached for the bread and said, 'It's a good job I like savoury food. Pass the butter, Ursh.'

Everyone laughed. Even Grandma after a few seconds. Will makes everything easy and fun. Especially Grandma. He's a miracle worker.

Saturday 21st January

Grandma and Will didn't stay in the end. That was good because we had an early start today. Shopping! Mum's early birthday present was a day to herself. Blane cried as we got in the car. 'She might be sad without us,' he said. I distracted him by asking what presents we should buy. I defo knew Mum wouldn't miss us. A whole day without noise and fights and crying and nappies and spilt food and fuss. Amazing!

The retail park is massive. At least, compared to the main street of Applemere, it is. And even though Dad gave us £10 each for Mum, I soon realised it wouldn't be enough. There was a blue top in a window that Mum would like, but it was £25. Then I saw a fluffy cushion, as big as her yoga ball that'd comfy when she'd been at the desk all day. But it was £19.99. I asked Dad if I could have more but he wasn't having it.

Spike spent ages in the candle shop. He smelt every flavour until he found the one. (Christmas Spice, half price in the sale.) Dad sent me outside with the pushchair because Harvest was getting restless. Blane kept bobbing in and out and then Kenny wandered outside too. I was left watching everyone while Dad and Spike looked at candles and Mum had her PJ day. I should charge them money.

One good thing happened. I convinced Kenny to put his money with mine so we could get the fluffy cushion. Mum will love it. I'll enjoy it too. With Grandma's tartan blanket and a massive cushion to sit on, my next film day will be epic.

Sunday 22nd January

After Friday Fooday and Saturday shopping, today was filled with horrible homework. (Loads of alliteration for you there, Auction Bidders!) I always leave things to the last minute. And it was Maths. Grrr.

Tea was root veg casserole and mash. The highlight of the day was the mash. It was not the page of linear equations I was still doing at nine.

Monday 23rd January

Mum is 41!

Jake almost missed the bus. He ran out of the mini supermarket and got onboard just as we were pulling away. When he got his breath back, he rooted in his bag and pulled out a present. 'From Mum and Grandad. For Molly.' He handed me a gift bag with some tissue covering the top but I could still peek underneath. Four cans of pink gin and a card. I panicked straight away. I'd get into loads of trouble if someone saw me with gin at school! I felt sick all through the journey. The winding country roads didn't help. Jake told me to stop stressing but that was easy for him to say. He didn't have alcohol in his bag.

When we arrived, I told Miss Wilkinson immediately. It seemed the best plan. It turned out, she wasn't bothered. She told me to put it in the stock cupboard until the end of the day. Problem solved. Sometimes I worry too much.

Mum was chuffed with the present. She's inviting Cait, Tom, and Jake to this week's Family Fooday. I predict a late night. She was also chuffed with her massive cushion. When I told her it was from me and Kenny, she laughed and said, 'It must be a coincidence that it's exactly what you'd want yourself.' 'Yeah,' I said. It must be,' and left it at that.

Tuesday 24th January

It's a family rule. The person whose birthday it is, chooses what we have for tea. This is brilliant when it's me, but not when it's Mum. She's the one who decided I was vegetarian before I was born. These days she's vegan. Mostly. I don't mind not eating meat (even though I had ham once and really liked it) but I *do* mind not eating cheese. Cheese is the best.

Last night Mum chose a pasta dish with roasted vegetables and a cheese substitute on top. *She* liked it. That was the main thing.

Tonight we finished the leftovers. It's still not my idea of a birthday meal.

Wednesday 25th January

Because I was thinking about ham, I messaged Jenna. The one time I ate meat was when her dad made me a sandwich and didn't know. It's funny thinking back, but I felt so guilty afterwards. Now, I'm not sure I would. I'd stand up for myself and tell Mum I'm old enough to make my own decisions. At least I would in my head. In real life, who knows?

I got the iPad after tea. Spike had been playing a game so this was a challenge all on its own. I pretended I needed it for homework. I don't feel guilty. Lying to brothers is normal. And he lies to me all the time. I'm owed a few fibs back. Jenna wasn't online so I wrote her a message about what I'd been up to since we chatted. It was mostly about school and how annoying Maths is. Hopefully she'll reply at some point.

Thursday 26th January

We finished Anne Frank in English. It was sad, even though the start of the story was like reading about someone like me. I wonder what Anne would've been like if she'd become a grown up. I wonder what I'll be like? Reading her diary made me see how lucky I am, even though small things annoy me. Whenever Harvest won't stop crying or Spike kicks the ball at my back when I'm watching TV, I'll think of Anne Frank. She'd put up with stuff like that if she could have her life back.

Friday 27th January

There'll be no time to write tonight because Jake's coming for Friday Fooday. I KNOW it'll be a late night.

Saturday 28th January

I was right. I got to bed at 1am! Mum tried to send me up earlier but then got sidetracked asking Cait if she could pull off an undercut. (IMHO, no.) It didn't matter. Me and Jake left the adults at the table (Mum, Dad, and Cait were on the red wine, Tom had whisky and water) and went to my room. If we shut the door, we could drown out the laughing from downstairs. 'Question!' Jake said, when we were comfy. 'Should I cut my hair? Mum's been nagging but I'm not sure.' I shook my head. His hair looks good. It flops into his eyes and he's always pushing it away, but it's so HIM.

When you think about it, Jake's quite good looking. In his living room, there's a photo of him and Cait from a couple of years ago. She looks the same but he's really little. Now he's taller, his face is older, and his shoulders are wider. Almost like an actual man.

We talked about the rest of Class 1. Jake said, 'Owen's OK but Lexi does my head in. She's always fiddling with her pen lid.' I hadn't noticed that but I let Jake moan. We all need it at times. 'I still don't chat to anyone in school apart from you,' I said. 'I wonder if it'd be different in a normal high school where there are more people.' Jake laughed and said, 'You ARE in a normal high school. What's normal, anyway?'

He's right of course. Normal is a pointless word. It means nothing. I feel normal in myself, but if I were normal like everyone else, I'd have less brothers and sisters, eat ham if I fancied, and definitely have my own phone.

Sunday 29th January

The problem with sharing the family iPad is you never see your messages. Jenna replied to me on Friday. Friday! I wasn't impressed. The first paragraph of my reply was a big apology. She'll understand. She was always good at knowing what my family's like.

She had lots of news but the biggest is that our old house has a new front door. 'Pale turquoise with a black knocker. Who do they think they are, McAuliffe?' I knew the new people would change things. But the fact it looks different on the outside feels strange. I'm glad I'm not there to see. It'd make my stomach churn.

Jenna's not spoken to Meg since Christmas. She's not in a strop or anything. 'Because I can't be faffed with the drama,' she said. I thought I'd know Meg forever but I'd honestly forgotten her until I read Jenna's message. We had good times in Primary school but that's over now. I'm glad she's in the past.

One day Jenna will come for a visit. I can't imagine what she'll make of Applemere.

Monday 30th January

I've made a decision. Just because Grandma said 'New Year, New You', doesn't mean I should spend all my time worrying about it. It's clear I can't find a new me if I haven't found the old one. Every time I've asked somebody, they've fobbed me off or made a joke. So as usual, I'm left to solve this puzzle on my own. I won't rush. I'll spend the rest of the year working out who I am, what I like, and what I'm good at.

Tuesday 31st January

I'd love to say tonight's tea was tasty and filling but I'd be lying. Mum was upstairs working for a new client, Harvest was playing up for Dad when it was time to sleep, and no one remembered to feed us.

I don't mean to brag but I saved the day. I thought about beans on toast – I could've if I wanted - but I was tired from school. So it was rice puffs and milk all round!

I also decided we should finish the shortbread from Grandma and Will. There was literally nothing Mum and Dad could say. If you forget to feed your kids, they WILL eat biscuits. That's just a fact.

2

Weirdness

<u>Wednesday 1st February</u>

The relief that Meg's in the past was short-lived. She's not been in touch, nothing like that. But there's another Meg in my life.

Poppy, the new girl, is exactly the same. Annoying and attention-seeking! (Sorry Meg, but that's how you were.) She acts like she's the boss of the class when she's only been here a month. I don't speak to her much because she's in the Y8 half of Class 1. We're in the same room for lessons but have different work. In Science she fake-laughed in James' face. It was SO loud. She really got on my nerves.

It's still annoying me, even though I'm in bed and it's been hours since it happened. I'm officially irritated. Grrrrrrrr.

Thursday 2nd February

Breaking News: I'm having another period! Mum said they might take time to settle at first so could come at any time. Today's the day! I have to count from when the last one started until now, and that's how long my cycle is. Some people's cycles are always the same but others are different. I counted. Mine was 34 days. I have a cycle!

The butterflies feeling is back. Like I'm nervous when there's no need. Mum said my hormones might make me feel sad and teary or grumpy and cross. I said I was fine.

Mum always talks about this stuff, which is good. How else do you learn? She's given me loads of tips. I need to keep pads in my school bag, I should make a note of what day my period arrives so I can work out when the next one might come, and if I get stomach ache I can have liquid paracetamol. So far, it's all OK.

Maybe THIS explains why I've been grumpy about Poppy. Perhaps she's a lovely person but I couldn't tell because of my hormones. I'm going to be double checking all my feelings from now on.

Friday 3rd February

I'm managing fine with periods in school. I just make sure I go to the toilet each breaktime. I keep wondering whether I was in a bad mood with Poppy for real, or whether it was my hormones. I watched her in registration. She was flicking balls of paper at Lexi. Lexi didn't mind - they've become friends - but I know if it was me, I'd be annoyed.

The good news was that Friday Fooday was gorge. Nut roast with veggies, potatoes, stuffing, Yorkshire puddings, and gravy. Mmm mmm mmmm. I went to bed full of food and feeling less annoyed with the world. Roast potatoes will do that to an almost-teenager.

Saturday 4th February

The weather's been rubbish lately. It's not like I love being outdoors but it's been raining for months and

I'm bored of staying in. I resigned myself to another Saturday of homework, noisy brothers, and a very noisy sister. It's not Harvest's fault she can only cry to get our attention but that doesn't stop it grating on me. (I thought that BEFORE hormones kicked in so it must be true.)

Cait's lent me a book. I like it when people suggest stories I might like. Her taste in clothes is very different from mine (lots of rips and black) but our book tastes might be similar. She left 'Twilight' with Mum the other day. She said, 'I wish this had been around when I was Leeza's age. Let's see if she's Team Edward or Team Jacob'. Mum says they're the names of the boys that want to go out with the main character, Bella. Except one's a vampire and one's a wolf.

Jake reckons Cait tries too hard to be a cool mum. I hope she doesn't give Mum any ideas.

<u>Sunday 5th February</u>
Homework all day. Boooooo.

Monday 6th February
Kenny is 4!

I got up early to see Kenny open his presents. He couldn't stop grinning! There were the usual things - socks, books, and a set of paints - but best of all, he got his own bike. Not even a hand-me-down! It's green, has stabilisers, and he loves it. When I left for the bus, he was riding on the landing and ringing the bell.

All day, I was excited to get home for Kenny's birthday meal. He'd asked last week. 'I want chicken nuggests and chips please.' That's how he said it. Nuggests. Mum said he could have plant nuggets instead. I was right to be excited. It was lovely. I dipped my nuggets (it's what we call them now) into BBQ sauce like I was on a fast-food advert. I know Mum and Dad try to give us home-cooked food but nuggets and chips might be my new favourite meal. THANK YOU, KENNY!

Tuesday 7th February
Even if I didn't like English, Ms. Phelps would still be the most fun teacher. This is because her hair is dyed bright red. If I knew nothing else about her, I'd know

she was fun from that. In today's lesson she told us we're doing a project on the language of fake news. We'll be put into mixed groups of Y7 and Y8. It'll last a few weeks ending with a presentation. It's the first time we've done something like this. I wonder who I'll be with.

<u>Wednesday 8th February</u>
ARRGGGHHHH. I'm with POPPY!

<u>Thursday 9th February</u>
Not just Poppy. Jake and Oscar too. Can you BELIEVE it? We've been put together because we live in the same village. I'm in the old farmhouse down the lane, Jake's above the mini supermarket, and Poppy and Oscar are on the new estate. Ms. Phelps said she'd grouped us so we could work together outside school. I am NOT comfortable with that. Jake's fine, but I can't have Poppy and Oscar witnessing the Crazy McAuliffe Chaos. (That's how Grandma once described our family.)

Our group sat together in double English. At one point, I put up my hand to ask a question, and under her breath, Poppy said, 'Yes Miss, please Miss, can I Miss?' in a stupid voice. It was noisy in class because we were discussing our projects, and Jake and Oscar were busy cutting out headlines. They didn't hear, but I did.

It is NOT period-grumps. She's the actual worst.

Friday 10<u>th</u> February

There's one upside to this project. I have to read online news stories. That means I get to hog the iPad every night. There's NOTHING Mum and Dad can say about it. Spike wasn't pleased when he realised. Ha!

After school I went to Jake's. It takes less than thirty seconds to get off the bus, cross the road, and walk through the mini supermarket to his flat. Tom waved from the counter as we passed.

Cait was folding her washing when I walked through the door. I knew it was hers because everything was black. 'How're you getting on with 'Twilight'?' she said. That threw me. I'm enjoying it but I don't like it as much as she does. 'It's great...,' I said, '... I never thought I'd enjoy a book about vampires...' I continued, '...but I suppose it's more about school and friends and boyfriends, really.' I thought that was a good response. Cait smiled. 'If I'd had a daughter, I'd have called her Bella. Like in the book. I love that story. Even though I'm well past high school and I prefer Edward's dad.' 'Don't get her started,' Jake said, and we went to his room.

Cait's been single for ages although Jake says she goes on dates now and then. I never think about mums having crushes. That's just weird. I never think about myself having crushes either. It feels like a confusing faff. When I was leaving, Cait passed me a DVD. 'Take this. Remember to check out the hot dad.'

One word. Yuck.

Saturday 11<u>th</u> February
I can't lie. The Twilight film was really good. And now I've seen it, I don't need to finish the book. Win.

Mum watched it with me whilst Dad took everyone up to bed. When it finished, she said, 'Go on then... Team Edward or Team Jacob?' I didn't really care but I said,

'Team Edward, I suppose. If I had to pick.' Mum nodded. Then she said, 'Team Carlisle. All the way.'

Urgh! Mum likes the vampire dad too! Why are adults being gross these days? Also, I wonder if this is where Bella from school got her name. I'm named after the eldest daughter from 'The Sound of Music' so maybe.

<u>Sunday 12th February</u>
After a lie in and some toast, I walked down the lane to return Cait's book and DVD. (I skim-read the rest of the book so I didn't have to lie that I'd finished it.)

When I arrived, Tom was in the kitchen. 'Have a seat, Leeza. Coffee?' I like Tom. He's the most grandaddy grandad ever. His thick white hair makes him look like Santa. Except he wears jeans and checked shirts every day. I said, 'No thanks. I don't like coffee.' That was true but I like that he offered me one. Like a grown-up. 'Jake's in his room. Mind you don't trip on the mess.'

I wasn't there long. We talked about the project. Jake had printed off some articles with dodgy headlines.

Ms. Phelps had said that when a headline tries to make you feel scared, it might be fake news. The first on the pile was DRINKING TOO MUCH WATER COULD KILL YOU. Fake news or not, Mum's always saying I don't drink enough water. I think I'm safe.

Something weird happened as I was leaving. Cait was at the kitchen table, drinking her coffee, when she said, 'Are you two doing anything for Valentine's Day?' Just like that. I went bright red and couldn't speak. Jake filled the gap by saying, 'God, Mum. Stop it!'

AS IF we'd be doing anything for Valentine's Day. Cait is **RIDIC**. I walked home all weirded out. And yet ten minutes earlier I'd been having a perfectly nice Sunday.

Monday 13th February
Just because a girl and boy are friends, does NOT mean they want to be girlfriend and boyfriend. I MUST have given Cait the wrong impression. I do NOT want to go out with her son. But being friends with him feels a bit weird now.

Poppy continues to get under my skin. She let the door shut in my face when we were coming in after break. I'm not taking it personally. I don't think it IS personal. She's a pain with everyone unless you're her mate.

Also, I keep saying WEIRD when I know it's only used when you can't think of a better word. It reminds me of Ms. Archer's Word Wall in Y6. She'd have put WEIRD at the top, then listed other options underneath. EERIE, STRANGE, UNREAL, CREEPY, SPOOKY, UNUSUAL, and BIZARRE.

Yep. Those are the words I'm feeling.

Tuesday 14th February

Jake got on the bus as normal. That was good. It made me feel normal too. He said, 'All right, Leez. Another pointless day of education awaits,' as he pushed his hair out of his eyes. He doesn't really mean that. He likes school. He's clever too. But I agree it can be pointless. Whenever I'm doing a subject I don't like I have exactly the same thought.

Obvs I didn't get any Valentine's cards which was a relief. I didn't send any either, so it evened out. In Maths, Lexi made James a home-made card. She ripped out the middle pages of her book when she was supposed to be working. I don't think she got round to converting many percentages into decimals. Not by my reckoning.

I'd calmed down by home time. I got on the bus in my own world, feeling happy I'd already done tonight's homework. As we set off, there was a tap on my shoulder. I turned to see Jake holding something behind my seat. I had to stretch round to see. 'We have a mystery,' he whispered. 'Who do you think this is from?'

Jake got a Valentine's card. And now everything feels weird again.

Wednesday 15th February

I can't stop thinking about the card. The writing was disguised and messy. I didn't recognise it. Jake said it was probably a joke but I don't think so. He's really nice. It makes sense that someone likes him. Even though it made me feel strange.

To stop thinking about the weirdness, I'm going to distract myself with my mind. Like this morning, when I pretended my burnt toast was pizza. That's when I realised I could do the same with other bad stuff. If anything uncomfortable happens, like Jake talking about the Valentine's card, or Cait making another comment, I'll laugh as if they've said something really funny.

We spent double English working on our group project. I pretended to laugh a few times. Every time Poppy made a joke.

Thursday 16th February
So far, I'm fake-laughing about the same amount as I'm real-laughing. Is that a good thing or not? School stuff is still weird (or eerie, strange, unusual) because of working with Poppy in English. I'll be glad when this project is over.

Home stuff is funny for real, though. At bedtime Kenny insisted on being carried up on Dad's back. Then Blane did. And then Spike. Spike pretended to be a jockey and kept shouting, 'Giddy up, horsey!' and, 'Trot on!' as Dad climbed the stairs. OK, when I write it down, I guess it's not *that* funny. At the time it was a nice distraction.

Friday 17<u>th</u> February
Break up for half term.

Grandma and Will were here when I got in. I'd forgotten they were coming, what with everything going on. At least I've got a week off school. Except I have to meet Jake, Oscar, and You Know Who to do our presentation. I'm not thinking about that yet.

After Friday Fooday finished, (veggie moussaka and crusty bread!) Dad and Will washed up, while me, Mum, and Grandma chilled in the living room. I say 'chilled' but Grandma's never chilled in her life. She sits too straight for that. At one point Mum was moaning about having stomach ache and said, 'Leeza knows about that now, don't you?' It took me a second to realise but then I twigged. Mum was having a period! I was part of the adult conversation. Like we were in a club! Grandma smiled. I thought she'd say something nice but instead she said, 'I'd offer my congratulations but it's nothing to celebrate. You have years of hell ahead. Good luck. I'm sure you'll be used to the drudgery of menstruation soon enough.'

So that was cheery.

Saturday 18th February
Slept in and did absolutely nothing. Well it IS the holidays.

Sunday 19th February
Same as yesterday.

Monday 20th February
Jake messaged. He'd been chatting to Poppy and she'd suggested meeting tomorrow. I know I have to. The presentation's got to be done the first Wednesday back and no one knows what they're doing. I told him tomorrow was fine but I'd prefer it not to be at my

house. He laughed. 'As if we'd get anything done with your lot running about,' he said. Jake always gets it.

One of the topics we have to cover is how social media promotes fake news. I know Jake doesn't care, and I'm sure Oscar isn't bothered, but something tells me Poppy will have opinions about my lack of phone and TikTok account.

Great. (That's sarcasm, Auction Bidders!)

<u>Tuesday 21st February</u>
We ended up at Jake's flat. He's in the village in the middle of us all. Besides, Tom was working in the shop and it was Cait's day in college. His place was empty.

Me and Oscar turned up with notepads. Jake had Cait's laptop so he could make our PowerPoint slides. Poppy brought her tablet and phone. She put them on the table like she was in a business meeting. It was hilarious but I couldn't say anything. She'd only tease me about not having my own.

Two things happened. Firstly, even though it was a pain giving up an afternoon of half term, we sorted out our presentation. We all know which bits we're reading and what'll be on the PowerPoint as we do. That's a relief. One piece of homework boxed off.

The other thing is, I know who sent Jake the card.

Wednesday 22nd February
It had to be Poppy didn't it. The one person I wouldn't want as his girlfriend. It was when she was doodling on her notepad that I spotted it. She switched hands so she was writing with her left and the capital G was exactly like the G in Jake's card. It said 'Guess who!' I don't need to Guess Who anymore. I know.

The next question is, do I tell Jake?

Thursday 23rd February
I'm thinking, no.

That wasn't all I thought today. I also wondered if Jake would still be my friend if he was seeing Poppy. What if she told him to ignore me? We'd have to be friends in secret and that'd be rubbish. Or worse, he might listen to her and turn against me. There are no good ways to look at this.

Friday 24th February

I didn't want to spend the last weekday of the holiday stressing about Poppy and Jake. So I made biscuits.

This looks like I've lost the plot. I've never made biscuits on my own before but I knew it'd keep my mind busy. Mum thought I'd lost the plot too. I said, 'I'm going to make biscuits for Family Fooday. Can I have some money for ingredients?' Her first response was, 'What's wrong?' which annoyed me. Why can't I make biscuits if I like? She must have seen my face because she didn't wait for an answer. She said, 'Sure. My card's in my purse. Do you know what you need?' I nodded. I'd already found an online recipe when I was on the loo this morning. I didn't tell her that. I can see it's gross when we share the iPad.

Jake wasn't in the mini supermarket which was a relief. That's the problem living in a small village. There's only one shop to buy ingredients. Tom scanned my flour, butter, sugar, and chocolate chips. 'Someone's baking,' he said. 'I'm doing biscuits,' I said. He walked around the counter and got a little bottle from the shelf. 'A teaspoon of vanilla will make them even better.' He put it in my bag without charging me.

With that random act of kindness, my whole day felt good. And even though I made a mess, and the biscuits at the back of the oven were burnt, I was completely distracted from the thoughts in my head.

And the biscuits were GORGE. The non-burnt ones, that is.

Saturday 25th February
I thought I'd take Tom some biscuits as a thank you but I had to act fast. When I got up, Spike had the tin from the cupboard and was piling up a tower. He was calling it a 'bicky-brekkie'. I shouted to Mum, who stopped him, then I wrapped three in foil. That way, Tom could choose to share with Cait and Jake. Or not.

It was freezing as I walked to the village. There's fields either side of the lane, so there's no shelter from the wind. I walked as fast as I could before making it inside the shop. I must've looked a mess. As soon as he saw me, Tom shouted upstairs, 'Cait, I've found a shivering urchin from the streets. I'd say she needs hot chocolate, now!' My cheeks warmed up just hearing that.

Tom was made up with the biscuits. He said he'd have one with his coffee. 'How's life at the old McAuliffe ranch?' he asked. He said it like a cowboy, which made me giggle. 'Mad as usual,' I said. 'Just as it should be,' he replied. Then he sent me up to get my hot chocolate.

That's when the bad thing happened. I was in Jake's room, chatting away. Everything was fine but then the project came up. Jake had been describing one of the PowerPoint slides to go with Poppy's part of the presentation. He finished by saying, 'It'll sound great on the day because she's good at talking confidently.' My cheeks started to burn. Not because of the cold this time. It made me mad the way he was bigging her up.

I couldn't help myself. I felt a rage inside that I had to let out. Without stopping to think it through, I said, 'You DO know Poppy sent you the Valentine's card, don't you?' It tumbled out of my mouth so quickly. I sounded angry. I think I WAS angry. Jake looked surprised for a few seconds but just smiled. 'Interesting,' he said.

I went home after that. I don't know what 'interesting' means and I don't know why Jake smiled. OMG. They're going to be boyfriend and girlfriend, aren't they?

Sunday 26th February
I'm running out of distractions. There's only so much you can do to forget things on your mind. I'm looking forward to school starting again. Even Maths will be a welcome break. That's how bad it is.

Monday 27th February
Dad is 43!
Back to school.

We piled into Mum and Dad's room first thing, to watch him open his presents. Last week Mum asked us what we wanted to get and she ordered the stuff online. That was easier than going shopping together. He was pleased with his herb garden seeds from Spike, his T shirt from me, and his underwear and socks from Blane and Kenny. Mum said that Harvest's present was that she'd promised to sleep right through tonight. Ha! I bet she doesn't.

Jake seemed normal. I kept staring at him and Poppy in class. I don't think he talked to her more than usual, but who knows what's happening secretly. Maybe they're messaging. Or writing notes to each other. I didn't see them do that but it doesn't mean they're not.

Dad's birthday food choice was - and thank goodness because I needed something to cheer me up - a chippy tea! The smell of chips makes everything feel better.

Tuesday 28th February
One more day before the presentation. It can't come soon enough.

I had an interesting chat with Mum after tea. I had brain fog (Grandma says that all the time) and I couldn't remember the word for when you date the opposite sex. It must be on my mind with the Jake and Poppy stuff. Mum reminded me it was called being straight.

It's such an odd phrase. Being straight. When Grandma tells me to sit up straight, it's uncomfortable. My shoulders ache, and I slouch as soon as she looks away. Would having a boyfriend feel uncomfortable? Like when I want to relax but I have to think of my posture?

That's why Grandma tells me to sit up straight. For my posture. I don't care about my posture. I don't even know what posture is. Once she said, 'Be thankful I'm not making you walk with a book on your head.' She does talk rubbish sometimes. I don't think I'm gay (which I know is the opposite of being straight) but I do want to relax my shoulders when I'm older. That's how I'll know I like someone.

I used to be able to relax my shoulders with Jake. Not that he's a boyfriend person. He's just a friend. At least he was until the weirdness started.

3

Do Your Best, Applemere

<u>Wednesday 1st March</u>

Pinch punch, first of the month! I'm not superstitious so I don't know why I wrote that. Anyway, whatever day it is, there was only one thing on my mind. The presentation!

We did a run through at lunch. It was fine. I just concentrated on my part. I'd planned to look up every so often and not stare at my lines. But that was too tricky. I'd rather read off the paper than look like I don't have a clue.

When double English started, Ms. Phelps made us move desks to make space at the front. That's when I realised some people were nervous. James looked like he was going to be sick. My first thought was, 'How ridic!' Then I felt sorry for him. My second thoughts are usually kinder.

When it was our turn, Jake opened the PowerPoint. 'Fake news was added to the dictionary in 2019 but the phrase was used long before then,' he began. He seemed confident. He's not shy but he's not loud either. It was strange to see him take charge and have everyone listen. Then it was my turn. I read out my page on the language of a fake argument. I used the DRINKING TOO MUCH WATER COULD KILL YOU example. Then Poppy described the role of social media in spreading misinformation. (Lots of people can read made-up things all at once.) Then Oscar shared ways to check if something is real. (Look at where it came from and who wrote it.) Then it was over.

The good news is, I never have to think about Poppy again.

Thursday 2nd March
OK, I know that's not true. Obvs I'll have to think about Poppy again. It's just nice that my days of

working with her are over. I watched her before registration. She was sitting on the desk with her feet on the seat. Lexi was looking up at her and laughing, like she was the funniest person ever. James, on the other hand, was sitting next to Lexi and still looked sick. Maybe it wasn't the presentation after all.

She saw me staring. I know that because she caught my eye then gave me a horrible look. For about 10 seconds. It's clear we're not meant to be near each other. Jake was in his usual seat facing the front and didn't see any of it. I'm still hoping his 'interesting,' comment about the Valentine's card didn't mean anything bad. When will things feel uncomplicated? **Argggghhh.**

(This house is too full to scream inside. I'm left with writing screams in my diary. I pressed extra hard for that one.)

Friday 3rd March
Jake got a message on the bus. He read it, burst out laughing, then handed me his phone. 'Tell your Mum

I'm not your personal secretary,' he said. Then he laughed again. It said...

CAN YOU TELL LEEZA TO PICK UP A BAG OF TORTILLAS, THREE TINS OF TOMATOES, AND SOME PEPPERS. THANKS! TOM KNOWS I'M PAYING TOMORROW. MOLLY X

Tom was waiting at the door as the bus stopped opposite. He handed over the bag before patting Jake's back. 'Another day at the coal face,' he said. They went inside and I was left to lug a bag of tins down the lane. All because Mum and Dad forgot they were making chilli. Ridic.

I got over it. Because something brilliant happened. The chilli was great - thanks to me - but while we were eating Mum said, 'I was thinking Leez, how about if Jenna came for a visit?' I thought I hadn't heard properly. I know it got mentioned when I saw her last year but parents say a lot of things that don't turn out later.

My smile must have filled the room. The thought of seeing Jenna made everything feel better. Mum said she'd message her dad. I know he'll agree. I can't wait to catch up.

In other news, if Mum needs me to do food shopping, she should buy me a phone. I'll choose my moment, but that's my most persuasive argument yet.

<u>Saturday 4th March</u>
My lie in was huge. I don't understand anyone who springs out of bed when they don't have to be up.

Spike was finally allowed to plant his seeds. Dad spent the morning with him outside, making a herb patch. 'Last year...' Dad said, '...I didn't plant enough. I know that now. You all laughed at my coriander but I'd only used one packet. This year, we'll be swamped!' Spike nodded, looked at the soil and said, 'If anyone gets on my nerves, they're not having my rosemary,' as he slapped his palm with the trowel. Dad put his arm around him like they were a united gardening team. Except later I heard him explain that they'd planted the herbs for the family and he couldn't pick and choose who ate them.

I'd forgotten last year's coriander. It was pathetic.

Sunday 5th March

I'm still waiting for Mum to message Jenna's dad. I must have gone on about it loads because at one point she snapped and said, 'One more time and I'm deleting his number.' I'd caught her at a bad moment. She'd been changing Harvest on her knee, while Blane was hugging her from behind, and Spike was shouting about defending his herbs in all weathers. I'd definitely misjudged my timing.

Monday 6th March

I told Jake about Jenna. 'No way, you've got another friend,' is what he said. Then he laughed. I pretend-punched his arm, which is exactly what Jenna would do in the circumstances. If we ever get the visit sorted, I'll have to introduce them.

I have no idea what either of them will think.

Tuesday 7<u>th</u> March

Dad made an announcement at breakfast. 'Ladies and gentleman, boys and girls, Harvest Sky McAuliffe would like to perform her new skill.'

We all trooped into the living room. Harvest was lying on her mat, looking at the ceiling. Dad knelt next to her and said, 'Go on Harvest, roll over. Roll for everyone, go on.' He kept repeating himself. For ages. It seemed her new skill was to ignore us and relax. But eventually she understood what Dad was saying. She had a bit of a stretch then pushed herself on her side. At first she rolled back. Then Kenny clapped and shouted, 'Go Harvest!' Spike joined in. 'Roll, roll, roll,' like he was cheering on a football team. A football team that rolls, that is.

In the end, it took 10 minutes of encouragement and lots of near attempts but finally, Harvest McAuliffe rolled from her back onto her front without any help from anyone. Well, apart from all the cheering and clapping. Just as she made it, Mum popped her head around the door. 'Jenna's dad said yes.'

I don't know if it was Jenna's visit or Harvest's roll, but the rest of the evening was full of happy feelings. It doesn't take much.

Wednesday 8th March
Period.
(There's no need to mention it anymore. Apart from writing down when it happens - so I can count the days - there's nothing else to add.)

Except today I came on in school. (That's what Mum calls it. Coming on.) And you know what? It was fine. I had the butterfly/stomach feeling at lunch, then at break I went to the toilet and realised. I nipped to my locker, got a pad from my bag, and put it up my sleeve. Then I went back to the loo and sorted myself out. Easy. I remember how much I dreaded starting my periods in school. In the end, it never mattered at all.

Thursday 9th March
Blane had the iPad all night. I complained to Mum but she said his homework takes longer because he's younger.

This makes no sense. Because he's younger, he has LESS homework. I have loads but I never get to hog it that long. Not that this was about homework. I was fed up because I wanted to FaceTime Jenna. We have a visit to plan.

In the end I sent her a quick message and we arranged to chat tomorrow evening. I've stuck a notice on the fridge. LEEZA HAS BOOKED THE IPAD FOR FRIDAY NIGHT AFTER TEA. No one's officially commented but I saw Mum raise her eyebrows when she was getting Harvest's milk.

Friday 10th March

I don't often want Friday Fooday to be over but I did tonight. As soon as I'd finished my pie (chickpea, feta, courgette!) I pointed to the fridge and reminded everyone I had an appointment. Mum usually stops us leaving the table before everyone's finished. On Fridays, at least. But I think she knew how frustrating it was when Blane was taking ages to spell.

A few minutes later, I was in my room and it was like old times. BRILLIANT old times. 'Yalright McAuliffe!'

was what Jenna said as soon as we connected. Then she blew her cheeks out and crossed her eyes, making a completely ridiculous face. I fell about laughing for the first five minutes. It was SO good to see her.

We talked for nearly two hours. Dad put his head round the door at 9pm to tell us to wind it up. It was just as Jenna was telling me about Meg and her boyfriend. Dad caught the words, 'I'm sick of them sucking face every ten seconds.' He stared straight at the screen for a moment before saying, 'Hello Jenna. It's so good to catch up.' Jenna burst out laughing and Dad left the room, giving me a five-minute warning.

But yeah, Meg's seeing someone called Rhys. He didn't go to Irwell Green Primary so I don't know him. When I asked if Meg had gone off Alfie Diggs, Jenna snorted. 'He's been suspended more times than he's been in.'

On the one hand, Meg and Alfie Diggs are as strange to me now as this Rhys guy. But on the other, it was so good to hear about people and places I used to know. The other good thing was we've booked a date for the visit. Two weeks and counting.

Saturday 11th March

Harvest rolls over all the time now. We've stopped clapping. I asked Mum what else the baby books say a 6-month-old should do. She didn't look up from the laptop. 'When you've had five kids in twelve years, the baby books are a waste of time.' This didn't answer my question. 'But what else will she do soon? What's next?' Mum carried on typing. 'Babies do what they like, when they like.' I sighed. I don't like not knowing things. Mum must've realised she was being annoying because she added, 'I s'pose we'll start her on solids soon.' Then she carried on with the spreadsheet.

I remember the solids phase from Kenny. It's when pooey nappies become even more disgusting. I've defo seen too much for my age.

Sunday 12th March

I made a list of fun stuff that me and Jenna can do. So far I've got...

- Friday Fooday
- Walk to the village
- Meet Jake

Then I got stuck. Applemere's boring when you write it down. I hope she doesn't regret coming.

Monday 13th March
We've got another project! It's OK. This one's to be done individually. Phew. I work better on my own. It's for History. We've got to interview someone about their life in the past. It can be anyone we know, but Mr. Khan said a grandparent is best. Then he added, 'Or anyone older than you,' because he remembered Owen's nan died at Christmas. Owen was fine but it was interesting to see how tactless Sir had been. It's not just kids who get things wrong.

I decided straight away. I had options, of course. I could interview Tom because he's just down the road, or I could FaceTime Will because it'd be a chance to find out more about him. But who am I kidding? There's only one option and I'll message her tomorrow.

Tuesday 14th March
Grandma's on board! She replied to my email straight away. 'It will be a privilege to describe my childhood

in detail and demonstrate how easy you have it today,' she wrote. She was probably being funny but you never know with her. I showed the message to Mum who sighed. 'She'll never shut up once she starts. Good luck, Leez.'

Wednesday 15th March
Jake's going to interview Tom. That makes sense seeing as they live together. Jake said he's already heard everything Tom will say, which also makes sense. I'm not so sure with Grandma. She talks a lot, but not about her past. Maybe I'll find out some family secrets. Or maybe her childhood was as boring as mine. We'll see. We're FaceTiming on Friday.

I know that because she emailed saying, 'I'll be ready for my closeup, Miss McAuliffe. 7 o'clock, Friday evening.' She thinks it's a fashion shoot, not an interview.

Thursday 16th March
We've got two weeks to do our history projects but I have to be organised. Grandma and Will are away next week. Like Mum said, it's only been two minutes since

their honeymoon. They're going to Paris for a couple of days, a week tomorrow. I cannot imagine going to another country for a weekend. It's the poshest thing I can think of.

Jenna emailed today. The subject was <u>ONE MORE WEEK UNTIL JENNA AND LEEZA'S EPIC WEEKEND OF FUN'</u>. When I read that, I laughed. Then I panicked. She's going to be disappointed. It's so different from Stockford. There's nothing here.

<u>Friday 17th March</u>
Another Friday evening, another booked appointment with the iPad. Dad lent me his phone so I could record the conversation. And wow, was that a good idea! I'd never have been able to keep up with all the talk. It felt like 5 minutes but we chatted for nearly an hour! After it was done, I typed up the opening thirty seconds. It starts like this...

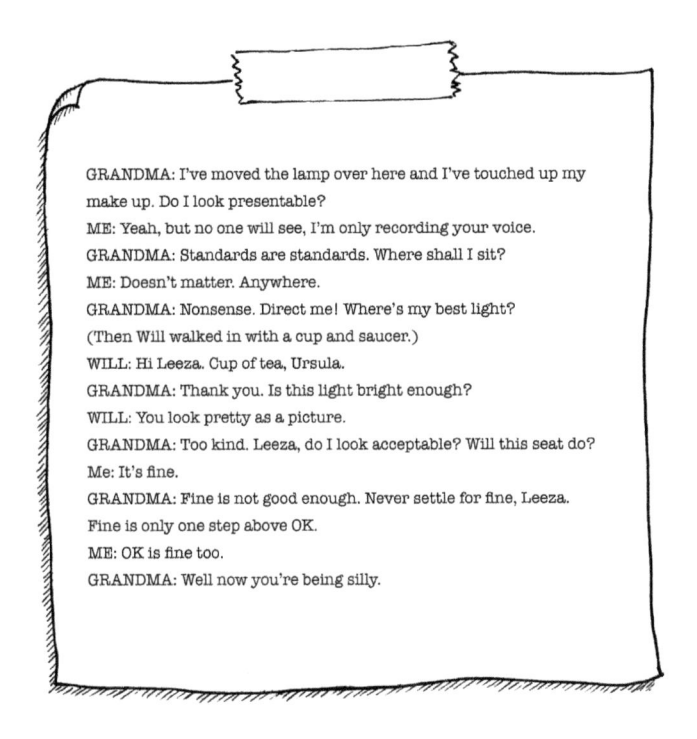

> GRANDMA: I've moved the lamp over here and I've touched up my make up. Do I look presentable?
> ME: Yeah, but no one will see, I'm only recording your voice.
> GRANDMA: Standards are standards. Where shall I sit?
> ME: Doesn't matter. Anywhere.
> GRANDMA: Nonsense. Direct me! Where's my best light?
> (Then Will walked in with a cup and saucer.)
> WILL: Hi Leeza. Cup of tea, Ursula.
> GRANDMA: Thank you. Is this light bright enough?
> WILL: You look pretty as a picture.
> GRANDMA: Too kind. Leeza, do I look acceptable? Will this seat do?
> Me: It's fine.
> GRANDMA: Fine is not good enough. Never settle for fine, Leeza. Fine is only one step above OK.
> ME: OK is fine too.
> GRANDMA: Well now you're being silly.

It went on like that for a while. I won't be including any of it in my report. It's nothing to do with history and everything to do with Grandma being ridic. Besides, for a grandma, she always looks good. I've never seen her with messy hair or without makeup. Not once. That's mad when you think about it.

Tomorrow I'll start typing the actual interview. It was fun in the end. Once she'd found the best light.

Saturday 18th March

I've never worked this hard at a weekend! Mum had to bring my lunch upstairs. It takes ages to listen to a recording and write it out. Dad told me it's called transcribing. People talk fast so there's lots of words. Especially Grandma. She talks faster than anyone when she gets going. Here's a bit about when she was young...

> GRANDMA: The war had been over for years but ration books were phased out when I was born. Tinned fruit was as fancy as we got. Not like today, with avocados and quinoa all over the place. Some families had lost men in the fighting, like Mrs. O'Malley next door. My father came home with a limp that lasted the rest of his life. He'd bang his stick on the floor whenever he wanted Mother's attention. Usually to make him a cup of tea. Sometimes she'd pretend she hadn't heard and he'd shout until she got up. I don't think they were madly in love, but they weren't unhappy either. They just got on with it. We had no television or Internet so it was the radio or nothing. I used to listen to Children's Hour every evening. My favourite food was jam sandwiches. It was the sort of thing you'd have for a party tea. When I was eleven, I passed an exam which meant I went to high school in another town. I'd walk to the station for half an hour every day. We didn't have a car because not every household did back then...

That's as far as I've got. She doesn't really stop for breath when she's talking about her childhood. And she jumps from one topic to the other without a break. I'll carry on tomorrow.

Sunday 19th March

I did a few more hours of transcribing after lunch. This was not a homework I could have left to the last minute. It takes so long! Here's a bit about her first husband, Mum's dad. It was harder to get Grandma chatting about this

> ME: What was he like?
> GRANDMA: Who?
> ME: My grandad.
> GRANDMA: A complete waste of space.
> ME: There must have been something you liked about him?
> GRANDMA: I suppose he had a sort of twinkle.
> ME: That's like Will. He has a twinkle too.
> GRANDMA: Will has a good twinkle. Your mum's dad's twinkle was a disgrace.

How can a twinkle be a disgrace? It was funny the way she said it. But then I remembered that in Y1, Caitlin Matherson used the word TWINKLE for her private parts. That made me burst out laughing. I'll tell Jenna about that when I see her.

Monday 20th March

Tom stopped by this evening. He's done a deal with Mum and Dad. If they teach him his new VAT software, he'll give them stock that's about to go out of date. He arrived with two multipacks of Monster Munch, three loaves of bread, and a couple of packs of cheese. Mum took him up to the office while Dad used the stuff to make tomorrow's packed lunches. I guess knowing stuff can pay at times.

When he was leaving, Tom said, 'Your mum has my sympathy, Molly. If Leeza's like our Jake, she'll have been grilled all week about her misspent youth.' Mum laughed and said, 'I can't see Ma having misspent anything.' He smiled and said, 'Ay, probably not. But it's been a lovely trip down memory lane, I can tell you.'

I wonder if Grandma enjoyed the trip down memory lane. She talked non-stop about being a little girl. But she was much less chatty about being a young adult. Perhaps her childhood was the best time of her life?

That's a really depressing thought for an 11-year-old to have. I'm waiting for life to get LOADS better than this.

Tuesday 21st March

I don't want 11 to be the best time of my life. That can't be true, can it? I live in the middle of nowhere, I'm overrun with siblings, and I have to book the iPad just to talk to my friends. It's got to get better than this. Hasn't it?

Wednesday 22nd March

More evidence that it's rubbish being 11. Mum told us at breakfast that we're cleaning the house later. When I asked why (it's not Christmas, and Grandma and Will aren't visiting) she told me it was for Jenna's visit. I nearly fell off my chair laughing. As IF Jenna cares about dust! Mum said she wasn't bothered whether Jenna cared about dust, but she did.

I knew what to say next. It's true so I couldn't get into trouble but I knew she'd go mad. I paused for a second before saying, 'You sound exactly like Grandma.'

Mum gasped. Actually gasped! Dad burst out laughing but stopped as soon as Mum glared. Being compared to Grandma is the worst thing I could say. In the end she took a breath and said, 'It's up to you. We can always cancel if it's not clean enough.' Then she got up and took her plate to the sink. Dad shook his head and smiled. I could tell he liked my joke.

I told Jake about Jenna's visit. He said, 'Cool. I get to meet your other friend. Is she like you?' I wasn't sure how to answer because I don't think she is. But I also know she's not like the girls at school either. She wouldn't be obsessed with James like Lexi, or think she's better than everyone like Poppy. Jenna does her own thing. 'Not sure,' I answered. Which is the truth.

Thursday 23rd March

I spent most of the evening tidying my room. Jenna's going to be sleeping on an airbed next to my bed. Tbf, it'll fit much easier now my junk's been shifted.

I might have hated the tidying but I'm really excited for tomorrow. I can't sleep! It's already midnight and I'm still thinking about the weekend. It all kicks off after school. Dad's picking me up then we're going straight to Stockford. He wants to get there before rush hour kicks in. We'll get Jenna, come straight back, and bring home a chippy tea. It's going to be a great Friday.

Friday 24th March
Today was a great Friday! I'm only writing a couple of sentences while Jenna brushes her teeth but I'll fill you in soon. We're having such a funny time. I feel like the me I used to be. It's great.

Saturday 25th March

Sunday 26th March

Monday 27th March
Auction Bidders, I'm back! Did you miss me? I'm in bed early because I'm shattered from all the fun. Here's what we did...

- We had a chippy tea for Friday Fooday.
- Jenna met Harvest and made her giggle so hard she was sick.

- I gave Jenna a tour of the house. She liked it, especially my room.
- She said, 'You could have a party in your bathroom it's that big!'
- I agreed but explained it's also draughty, has a toilet with a dodgy flush, and a bath that I won't use because of all the gunk. (It's still on Mum and Dad's To Do list.)
- On Saturday we walked to the village.
- Jenna met Jake.
- They both hit it off – by talking about me.
- Tom gave us free crisps and pop.
- We chatted on the benches outside the pub.
- Jenna said, 'I hope you're looking after my McAuliffe, Jake. I don't want to have to turn nasty.'
- Jake said, 'As you're the scariest person at this table, I'll do exactly as you say.'
- They carried on talking about me like I wasn't there. (I quite liked it.)
- Later, I told Jenna about Poppy. She said, 'What a cow,' more than once.
- Jenna asked me if I wanted to go out with Jake.
- I said no.

- But I added that I didn't want him seeing Poppy either.
- Jenna said she can't stand boys like that. Only as friends.
- I agreed. I like Jake but not like that.
- We had a BBQ in the garden!

The BBQ was the best part. Defo. When it's warm, Mum makes us eat outside. We can spill crumbs and there's no need for the dustpan and brush. But this BBQ wasn't like that. It was a properly organised outdoor meal. We cooked veggie burgers and Dad lit the firepit. I didn't know we had one. There's been a rusty metal bucket at the bottom of the garden since we moved in and apparently that's it! We had to search for all the broken twigs, put them in the bucket, then he set them on fire. He added a few logs from the fireplace too. It was brilliant. Really warm and cosy. We sat around it like a campfire.

Me and Jenna stayed outside until dark. My shoulders were definitely relaxed. With the sky full of stars and the fire crackling away, it was actually amazing. At one point, Jenna lay back in her deck chair and said, 'This is like a proper holiday, McAuliffe. It must be amazing to live here all the time.' I don't know if she's been away since we moved, but she never went on holiday when we lived nearby. I'm glad she had a good time. I felt proud of Applemere.

That's something I never thought I'd feel when we moved here. It's funny how things change.

Tuesday 28<u>th</u> March

I feel a bit down since Jenna's gone. I know that's normal after having a good time, but it's no fun. Jake was nice today. He said, 'How are you managing now I'm your only friend again? Can you cope?' I knew he was joking so I gave him a push. I like that we can tease each other without being mean. I think that's what friends can do. It's how me and Jenna are, all the time.

Mum's invited Cait, Tom, and Jake for tea on Friday.

Wednesday 29<u>th</u> March

Poppy's been at it again. In English we had to work in pairs. Before Ms. Phelps had finished speaking, Poppy had moved her chair over to Jake so he had no choice.

I watched them this afternoon. They were supposed to be working even though Poppy spent more time pretending to laugh at everything Jake said. I know him. He's not THAT funny.

I found myself telling Mum about it after school. It spilled out when she asked me about my day. 'He'll work it out soon enough,' is what she said. 'What if he doesn't, then they go out together, and she turns him against me?' I really did let it all out. Mum thought for a moment. 'If he's that quick to ditch his friends, you're probably best off without him, aren't you.'

I know that makes sense. But as he's my only mate in school, it's not a great plan.

Thursday 30th March

Poppy sat next to Jake at lunch. I walked into the room, saw he was busy, so chose another table. He didn't see me so it's not like he chose her over me. It still felt like that, though.

In other news, Mum's called a family meeting. She told us at tea time. 'Sunday afternoon, kitchen table, be there or be square.' My heart sank. They're never about sharing good news. The last couple were when she told us she was pregnant with Harvest, and when she announced we were leaving Stockford. Now those things have happened, I guess they've turned out OK. At the time they felt awful. Like everything I knew for certain was changing. With Jake being weird and Poppy taking him away, it's not been a good day.

Friday 31st March
Friday Fooday was supposed to cheer me up. Instead, everything felt off. We had pasta bake with spinach, halloumi and tomatoes. Dad had made bread and Tom brought a lemon drizzle that was just past its sell by. At least the meal part of the evening was good.

Me and Jake left everyone at 8pm and came to my room. The airbed's still up since Jenna, so he slouched on that while I sat on my bed. He knew something was wrong. 'What's up with your face?' he said. I wasn't pulling a face but he still knew. 'Nothing,' I said. 'Don't believe you,' he said. It could have gone on like that for ages. In the end I thought I'd just say it. 'Poppy's doing my head in,' I said. He looked blank for a second before saying, 'Poppy from school?' Like it could have been one of several Poppys. 'Yea-ahhh,' I said, but I sang it like I was teasing him for being stupid. He shook his head. 'I know she can be annoying but she's harmless. Just ignore her.'

That was what made me mad. Being told to ignore someone I'd just explained was annoying me. Why **SHOULD** I? Why wasn't I **ALLOWED** to be annoyed? I did my best to keep my temper but I could tell my voice sounded angry. 'Just because she sent you a Valentine's card, doesn't mean you have to defend her. You're allowed to think for yourself, you know.' He shook his head and said, 'I've no idea what your problem is. The card was nice but it doesn't mean anything. It was just a bit of fun.'

Jake doesn't understand anything. Poppy isn't fun. She's horrible. Why can't he see that?

4

More-Happy Than Not-Happy

<u>Saturday 1st April</u>

Today has been filled with homework. Rubbish. Oh, and I've just remembered. It's the family meeting tomorrow. Great. (That 'great' is extremely sarcastic, btw. I'm sure you worked that out.)

<u>Sunday 2nd April</u>

I woke up in a bad mood. I know this because I snapped at Dad when he asked if I wanted toast. 'Of course I want toast, it's breakfast,' is what I said. He didn't mind. 'Someone's woken up on the wrong side of bed this morning,' he said, as he passed me a slice. I brushed it off but felt irritated inside. Not about the toast. That wasn't anything. It was the family meeting hanging over me.

Every family meeting has the same rules. Any of us can announce one. They only happen at 3pm on a Sunday, and we've all got to be there. We must listen to whoever's speaking and be polite at all times. Last year, when they told us we were moving, I lost my temper. It's hard to be polite when your whole world's turning upside down. With that in my memory, you can see why I felt stressed.

Mum has a saying. 'It's always better than you think it'll be.' She said it to Harvest before her last injections, which was pointless because Harvest didn't know what was happening. I'm not sure it's true every time.

This time, however, she was right. It WAS better than I thought it'd be. The family meeting that is. Too tired now from all the stress. I'll fill you in tomorrow.

Monday 3rd April

Right then. The big announcement? Mum and Dad are having a party. It's for Harvest. They're calling it a naming ceremony. 'Like a christening?' asked Blane. He's been doing christenings at school and looked proud that he'd been able to add something. Most of the time, the family meetings are Mum and Dad talking and us listening. (Actually, just Mum talking.) 'Exactly like a christening except without the church or vicar. We thought we'd have it in the garden. It's our first party in Applemere so it needs to go with a bang, not be a damp squid.' I'd never heard that saying before. Damp squid. I'll have to work it into conversation.

Mum was enthusiastic but I had my doubts. Not that it isn't a nice idea. And it was a BIG relief that it was nothing worse. But the garden? It's an overgrown mess! We only have six garden chairs and Spike's territorial about his herb patch. If anyone goes near it, he'll kick off! They haven't thought this through.

Tuesday 4th April

The good news about the party is that it's given me a safe topic to discuss with Jake. Other areas of convo feel dodgy. Obvs Poppy, but school in general as well. I needed to get things back on track and Harvest's party did the trick. 'Am I invited?' was his first question. I said he was. Not that I know for sure, but if Mum and Dad want a party to welcome Harvest to the world, they have to invite the people that were there for her arrival at the Harvest Festival.

I wonder if Harvest will grow up thinking there's a festival named after her?

Wednesday 5th April

Blane and Kenny have begun making plans. They were drawing their ideas on Blane's doodle pad before bed. Most were hard to work out but I spotted a cake and a bubble machine.

Kenny's learning to write his name. It's a big achievement for someone left to watch cartoons while Mum and Dad work. He'd done Ks all over the page and Blane had tried to spell 'nuggests'. With nuggests, cake, and bubbles, there's no more planning needed. (More sarcasm, FYI.)

Thursday 6th April

It's funny. Sometimes everything's OK but other days I'm raging inside. Just looking at Poppy today made me want to scream.

It happened in English. I was answering Ms. Phelps' question about a character. I said, 'He wants everything exciting and fun, and not be a damp squid.' That's when Poppy piped up. 'Damp squid? It's damp SQUIB!' Then she laughed in a really horrible way.

Ms. Phelps was kind. She ignored Poppy and agreed with my answer, but when I checked later, Poppy was right. What's a damp squib? What does that even mean? And even if it's squib and not squid, a squid lives underwater so would be damp all the time. I decided I hated her then. DEFO. I know my face was bright red. **ARGGGGGGGH**.

The only good thing is that Jake had gone to the toilet. He missed me looking stupid in front of everyone.

Friday 7th April
Break up for Easter.

The naming party has been set for two weeks' time. I'm giving this my full attention to forget about yesterday. As predicted, there's loads to do. Mum and Dad told us the chores over tea. They'd cooked nuggets and chips. This was clearly a bribe to get us onboard. Although it worked with Kenny. He was made up to have a repeat of his birthday meal.

The main goal is to get the garden nice. They've put Spike in charge, which is a mistake. They want to keep him happy and the garden is his calm place. With him bossing us around, it'll get uncalm very quickly.

My job is to design the invitations. I'm allowed to use Mum and Dad's work computer so they'll look proper. Not just felt tips and handwriting. I'm happy with that.

It's a good job we've broken up for the holidays. There's so much to do. And that's before you count the homework I've been given. I don't often miss Primary School but when I think how much homework I've got, I wish I was back. There'd be no Poppy in my face either.

Saturday 8th April
Spike needs to calm down. He gave me a list of garden jobs the second I came downstairs. On the first day of the holidays too. Mum told him we'd do our best, then

whispered to me, 'Just let him think he's in charge even if he's not.'

I don't think I can manage that. Why should I have to listen to an 8-year-old? I ignored Mum and went to have a shower. Later I heard Dad say to him, 'The best way to get people to do what you want is to be kind and friendly.' Impossible. Spike would have to change his entire personality.

Sunday 9th April
Two events might happen soon. I'm predicting them both. First of all I felt the fluttery feeling in my tummy. I counted back the days and my period is on its way. Check me out! I'm getting organised these days.

The second event is well funny. Unless you're Spike. According to Dad's weather app, it's going to snow!

Monday 10th April
Period – just as I said.

Spike spent the whole morning shouting about the weather. It wasn't even snowing, just colder that it'd been. When Dad said they might have planted the herbs a bit early, Spike looked like he was going to cry. I felt sorry for him then. Last I saw of the plants, they were being carefully replanted into big pots and moved to shelter by the back door. He's definitely kind and friendly to shoots!

Mum was straight onto the two-week forecast. It hadn't occurred to her that April in the Lake District mightn't be the best time for a garden party. Tbf I'd also assumed winter was over but as Tom said last week, 'Ne'er cast a clout till May's out.' I checked this online so I could spell it right. (I can't have another 'damp squid' experience.) When I asked what he meant, Tom said he wasn't sure but it was something to do with jumpers. That makes sense because I wore my Christmas jumper all day.

Tuesday 11th April
Still no snow but I stayed in the warm.

Mum told Cait about the naming party. I could hear her through the phone, as well as Tom shouting in the background. They were very loud. 'We'll get the folding chairs from the village hall,' Tom yelled. 'That's apt considering it's where she was born,' said Mum. 'What a night!' said Cait, as Mum raised her mug in the air. 'You're telling me!' she said. Then they all laughed.

I listened in disbelief. A baby arrived in a village hall, with no medical help for ages. I know Cait's a nurse but she didn't have any stuff with her. And Billy's window van was no substitute for an ambulance. Meanwhile the rest of us were waiting outside till all hours, not knowing what was going on. And they think it's funny! I'm the only person who sees things properly.

Wednesday 12th April
'I'm the only person who sees things properly' is exactly the sort of thing that Grandma would say. I groaned to myself when I realised. (But it's true.)

Jake was here this afternoon. He said, 'Mum's doing her assignment and said to make myself scarce.' Cait's studying for a degree on top of her nurse job which Mum says is very impressive. I thought about that when I opened my school bag and decided my homework could wait. If I had a job and had left school, there's no way I'd be doing extra. Even if it was a fun subject.

Jake was also impressive today. He'd done research and had questions about the party. 'Will it be a civil-naming ceremony?' was one of them. How grown up does that sound? I was gobsmacked. (I LOVE that word!) Apparently there's a legal thing you can do to make it official. Mum looked taken aback. She said, 'To be honest, Jake love, it's just an excuse for a knees-up. Let's not get bogged down in the details.' Jake laughed and said, 'Righto Molly. You're the boss,' and then spent the rest of the afternoon sharing his ideas. They mostly involve letting off balloons and getting everyone to write down a wish for Harvest's future. He was getting well into it.

I've still got to do the invites. They have to go out soon.

Thursday 13th April

The computer is being used today but not tomorrow. Tomorrow's a Bank Holiday and Dad said no one'll be at work. Anyone they need to email, has to be today. That's OK. I can wait until tomorrow and I've already planned the design. At least I thought I had.

This was what I'd decided. Imagine Harvest. If you don't know her, she looks like a baby. Wispy hair, a soggy smile, and she waves her hands in the air when she's trying to roll. Think of a photo of her with a thought bubble coming out of her head. It says, WHAT'S MY NAME? At the bottom, it says, FIND OUT AT HARVEST'S NAMING CEREMONY. ON THE 22nd APRIL AT THE FARMHOUSE.

I thought that was great. Except Jake pointed out the problem. 'You've already told everyone Harvest is called Harvest on the invite. And she knows her own name. She just waved at me when I said, 'Hi Harvest.'

I'll have to rethink. I won't sleep now.

Friday 14th April

Mum put her head around my door this morning. 'You're too old for Easter eggs now, aren't you.' I'd just woken up so I couldn't answer. And she said it like a statement, not a question. Am I too old for Easter eggs now? I didn't think so. I know I'm almost a teenager but I didn't think Easter eggs were something you grew out of. Does having periods mean I'll stop wanting chocolate? I hope not!

It's only Grandma that gets us Easter eggs. And Irwell Green Primary used to give everyone a Creme Egg on the last day of term. Mum and Dad never bother. Mum says it's because we're not religious, as if that makes it OK to deny their children chocolate when everyone else is stuffing their faces. We aren't seeing Grandma for Easter this year because she's coming to Harvest's party instead. Two weekends in a row is too much travelling. I get that, but it's sad that we'll miss out on our only chocolate egg.

I made the invitations this afternoon. Now the speech bubble says, I'M HARVEST. COME TO MY NAMING CEREMONY! They look great, even if I say so myself.

Saturday 15th April
Mum took me, Harvest, Kenny, and Blane on a walk to post the invitations. It was to get us out of the way so

Dad and Spike could jet wash the patio. They were taking it far too seriously. Dad said, 'This is men's work,' and puffed his chest out with his hands on his hips. Mum said, 'I prefer men not to rely on restrictive gender stereotypes to make themselves feel important.' Dad laughed and went back to normal. That means he stopped having a puffed-out chest with his hands on his hips and stopped pretending to be bossy. All the while, time was ticking and we were still waiting to leave the house.

We put invitations through the doors of people who were there when Harvest was born. Josie the doctor, Billy the window guy, and Doris. She waited with us all night, even though the festival was over. And Tom, Cait, and Jake, got theirs, of course. They were the most helpful when it all kicked off. Then we put Grandma and Will's, Will's daughters' and Jenna's in the post box. I already know Jenna can't come because her Dad's working, but I wanted to show her the finished design.

When we got back, the patio was spotless. It's now creamy beige instead of murky grey. Amazing. Then I noticed the brick walls. All the grime from the ground was splattered up the back of the house. Mum gasped when she saw it. Then she laughed and said, 'It seems you've got a bit more men's work to take care of.'

In the end it was a family effort. We all tried the jet wash. It was the best fun. Even Blane and Kenny managed with Mum's help. The walls are now as clean as the patio. Dad said, 'Team work makes the dream work.' Except my dream is to go on holiday to a beach. Not to have a tidy back garden and mud-free walls.

Sunday 16th April
Happy Easter to those that celebrate. Grandma texted Mum this morning to say, 'I wish you all a peaceful day.' Mum snorted, read it out to Dad, and said, 'Fat chance. It's like she's trolling us.'

It might not have been peaceful but there was a lovely surprise after dinner. Tom turned up with a bin bag. He said, 'No point them being on the shelves now,' and opened it to reveal... Easter eggs! Tom is the BEST! We got to pick one egg each. I chose the Wispa one. It was huge. Bigger than a Creme Egg, anyway. Blane and

Kenny picked the Buttons ones and Spike chose the Flake. Mum said we could open them after tea.

I enjoyed my veggie lasagne with a side of roast potatoes but I loved my Wispa egg. Am I too old for Easter eggs now? The answer to that is, 'Absolutely not!'

Monday 17th April

There's a list on the fridge stuck under a Quarry Bank Mill magnet. It says MCAULIFFE FAMILY JOBS at the top. I rolled my eyes the first time I saw it. Whenever I go past, it reminds me that for all Mum says about supporting people who are unfairly treated, she'll still use her kids as unpaid workers.

I had to clean the skirting boards. All afternoon. Every single bit in the whole of downstairs. My knees are killing from the hard floors and my back's aching from bending down. I guarantee not a single person will notice. Even if they did, they wouldn't care.

I tried to say this to Mum but she was having none of it. And it could be worse. Blane was given the task of pulling up the weeds between the paving stones. It's freezing outside. When he came in, his hands were bright red and his teeth were chattering.

Tuesday 18th April

The weather app says that Saturday will be 13°C and dry. Mum reckons that's jacket or cardy weather. I'm not so sure. It was 8°C and dry today which is only 5 degrees less, but I was still freezing.

This evening, Tom and Jake turned up with a measuring tape. They wanted to see if one of the gazebos from the village hall would fit at the bottom of the garden. I've no idea what the answer was because I was inside, out of the wind.

Apparently, there's no wind planned for Saturday. Mum will say anything to shut me up.

Wednesday 19th April

Even though it's the school holidays, Mum and Dad are still at work. When they were at Stockford council they took time off to look after us. Now we've moved and they work upstairs, they work even when we're off school. Every so often they take it in turns to stand at the top of the stairs and shout, 'Any problems?' It's not exactly hands-on parenting but so far, it's working.

The list of chores is to keep us busy. Today when they shouted, 'Any problems,' they got Spike shouting, 'Kenny won't follow my orders,' they got Kenny shouting, 'Spike's a poo face,' and they got Blane having a meltdown because he was missing his teacher. I didn't shout back. Maybe I'll wait till the last day of the holidays and give them a list of the gripes I've collected over the fortnight.

Or I'll probably just get on with it. Like I usually do.

Thursday 20th April

I made a start on my homework. It gave me an excuse to get out of washing the bits of food from the clean knives and forks. Dried-on broccoli is fine if it's just us, but when there's real guests, it's gross.

Dad and Blane cleaned the cutlery while I stayed in my room and did a couple of worksheets. I still love English but answering questions about relative clauses is not the same as reading a good book. Let's be clear about that.

Friday 21st April

There's no way tomorrow will be cardy weather. The temp's down to 6°C! Tom arrived first thing with chairs in the back of a van. He was wearing a coat over his jumper, and a shirt and vest. (I heard him telling Dad.) Cait and Jake helped unload the chairs into the back and lined them up into rows. Mum and Dad spent the day in the kitchen. My job was hiding clutter in the hall cupboard and forcing the door shut.

Tom has also lent us the outdoor lights from the village hall. They're strung along the main road at Christmas and it takes a team of volunteers to put them in place. With just Tom, Cait, and Dad, it was a right faff to get them hung in the garden. I did my History and some of my Science in the same time. But when I was walking upstairs just now, I looked outside. The lights looked like a twinkly canopy, as if the whole garden has a sparkly roof. The gazebo we've borrowed is at the bottom of the garden with lanterns inside, ready to be lit. I stood looking for a few minutes. It's magical. I've come to bed feeling warm and cosy.

Whatever happens, I'm sure tomorrow will go well.

Saturday 22nd April
Argggghhhhh. It snowed in the night!

I've just woken up and I'm getting yelled at to help. Mum's stress is off the charts. Auction Bidders, I'll fill you in when I can. Today is going to be a nightmare.

Sunday 23rd April
Oh my days. To describe yesterday as 'panic stations' doesn't do it justice. Mum was shouting at everyone to get up and help without telling us what help was actually needed. Dad was telling us to calm down, even though it was only Mum that needed to do that. Kenny wet himself for the first time in ages and Spike couldn't stop being loud for no reason. I took myself away from the flapping and had a shower. It seemed best.

While I was getting dressed, I could hear a rumbling sound. I went to the window as it got louder. Then I saw. At the top of the drive, Tom and Jake appeared. They were pushing a big wheelbarrow which was carrying Cait! She couldn't stop laughing and nearly fell out every time they went over a pothole.

'We've brought salt!' Tom announced as Dad opened the door. I thought he'd gone mad but Mum said, 'Tom, you legend! You've saved us all!' It turns out that putting salt on the snow stops it going slippery. By the time the guests turned up, the driveway was covered in it, the chairs had been dried off and were dotted about inside, and the gazebo for the food, had been moved outside the back door, like an extension to the house.

Grandma arrived at 3pm wearing a hat. Like she was at a wedding or getting a medal from the King. Her opening words were, 'Molly, what a disaster!' which was really funny when you think about it. Even if something IS a disaster, it's the last thing you say out loud, isn't it? I thought Mum would lose it. She'd been in a mad whirl all day but by then, she was calmer. (Cait had poured her a gin.) She said, 'Ma, Harvest's naming ceremony is exactly like her birth. A real community effort. Come and meet everyone.'

The naming ceremony still happened but with a bit of a rethink. Jake's balloon idea hadn't been possible - the burst rubber is bad for cows. Instead he was in charge of the 'Wish For Harvest' jar. People had to fill out a slip of paper, saying their wish for Harvest's life. Mum played her birthing playlist because as she said, 'It was sod all use on the night, what with me forgetting to press play.' Then Grandma and her hat did a speech. She began, 'My fifth grandchild may as well have been born in a Bethlehem stable such was the humble nature of her surroundings,' which some people found funny but made Mum and Dad stare hard at each other. She carried on, 'But manger, hay bale, Harvest festival, or BUPA hospital ward, we're very grateful she's here.' Tom shouted, 'You don't get Billy's van on BUPA,' and everyone laughed for real. Including Mum and Dad. I did too, even though I don't know what BUPA means.

Jake wanted to hand over the 'Wish For Harvest' jar but I still hadn't done it. 'She's your sister, it should be easy,' he said. In the end I went to the loo (TMI) because I wanted thinking time. She's to open it when she's 18 (as if a glass jar will survive that long round here!) so it needed to be a grown-up thought. What do I wish for Harvest? I suppose the same things I wish for myself.

In the end I wrote, 'MY WISH FOR HARVEST IS... that you feel more-happy than not-happy, every single day.' At first I was going to say, 'That you feel happy every single day,' but I've realised that's not realistic. Feeling not-happy is something that will happen sometimes. And that's OK.

I went to bed shattered but relaxed. Me and Jake seemed back to normal, and it was nice to hear Doris' stories and Billy's singing again. I slept well last night.

<u>Monday 24th April</u>
Back to school.

Applemere snow is snowier than Mancunian snow. FACT. It's thick and goes nowhere. In Stockford, the streets would be full of kids and the pavement would be empty because of the snowball fights.

Even though I crossed my fingers all night, school was still open. The bus route had been salted, and the snow plough had come through Applemere in the night.

That's one difference between the countryside and the town. I'd never heard of a snow plough before we came here.

Tuesday 25th April

It's starting to thaw but still freezing. When the bus was late, I thought I would cry it was so cold. Then Jake beckoned me inside his shop and we waited behind the Kinder Egg shelf. When the bus finally arrived, we had to dash outside without slipping on the ice. It was an energetic start to the day.

Tea was homemade hummus, pittas, and veggie sticks. Mum and Dad never get cold weather teas right.

Wednesday 26th April

Harvest rolled not once, not twice, but three whole times. Technically I was in charge of her. Mum and Dad had taken everyone else up to bed but I was looking at photos on the iPad so I didn't pay her any attention. Sorry Harvest. I hope this hasn't made your day not-happy.

Thursday 27th April
I got my Maths homework back with a 'See Me' comment. When I spoke to Miss Wilkinson at the end of the lesson, it turns out I'd completely misunderstood the exercise. She said, 'I know you find Maths difficult but you're normally better than this. Is there anything going on at home that's making things hard?' I nearly did a Mum and snorted in her face.

Is there anything going on at home that's making things hard? WHERE SHALL I BEGIN?

Friday 28th April
I know Miss was being nice but the question really annoyed me. She thinks the reason my homework was rubbish is because my parents fight, or I'm getting beaten up, or there's a massive family drama I can't talk about. If I told her the real reason my homework isn't great, she'd lose sympathy. I have valid reasons but they don't count in the sympathy stakes. Trust me. I know.

Saturday 29<u>th</u> April

For the record, here are the reasons my Maths homework was wrong.

- I don't get Maths. (That's the biggest reason tbh.)
- There's no one at home to help me.
- I spent the holidays working through a list of party chores that took up all my time.
- I'm left to watch Harvest a lot, especially when we're off school. And Spike, Blane, and Kenny too, for that matter.
- It's impossible to concentrate on homework when Mum and Dad are working and I'm left to split up fights and stop Harvest from screaming the place down.

See? No one cares about that. Not a teacher, that's for sure. As long as I'm safe and being fed, they've done their duty. It's a nightmare. My brain works best when I'm alone in silence but I live in a house with loud people and chaos.

One day, I'll have my own flat, with no one else in it. Not even a goldfish. That should have been the wish I had for Harvest too. Except she might like people and loud things. Who knows?

<u>Sunday 30th April</u>
One more sleep until my birthday month. I should ask for my own flat without a goldfish. You never know? It could happen.

5
Adults Need To Adult

Monday 1st May
Bank Holiday.

I asked Dad why we had a day off. He said, 'Because that's what they did years ago.' He says that when he doesn't know something.

Tuesday 2nd May
I found out the answer. During registration, Miss Wilkinson said, 'I hope you enjoyed your long weekend?' and Lexi shouted out, 'Why do we even have Bank Holidays anyway?'

What I liked was that Miss didn't know either. It's annoying when adults pretend they know everything but make it up as they go along. She said, 'Excellent question Lexi, I'm not sure. Let's look it up.' She got on her laptop and brought up Wikipedia. It seems the reason we have Bank Holidays is because years ago, someone decided banks should have a day off. Then it spread.

It seems Dad was accidentally right. (He defo didn't know for real.)

Wednesday 3rd May
My Maths homework came back. I still got some wrong but I didn't have to 'See Me'. Perhaps Miss Wilkinson realised there's no point. I'm never going to be a Maths teacher and there are no other jobs where you need Maths every minute. When I'm an adult with a phone, I'll have a calculator with me. My brain can stay number-free.

Mum and Dad have been in weird moods. When I got back, they were at the kitchen table instead of in the office. Dad was staring into space and Mum looked furious. I wonder what Grandma's done now?

Thursday 4th May

There's a strange atmosphere at home. No one's cross or shouty but it's like we've had a row and not made up yet.

I know I'm fine and I'm pretty sure it's business as usual for Spike. After tea, I watched him go outside, lie on his tummy, and talk face to face with the herbs. Blane had five spellings to learn so he was writing them out on his notepad. Kenny was tired during tea so went to bed early and Harvest had a whinge before being taken up around seven.

So far, my detective work has eliminated all the kids. The weird strangeness has GOT to be coming from Mum and Dad.

Friday 5th May

I watched them at breakfast. They didn't say a word to each other and not many more to us. It's not as if they row. Some parents are always kicking off, but Mum and Dad get on. I've never seen them like this.

Except I have. The last time Mum was quiet and not herself was when she found out she was having Harvest. It's exactly like that.

OMG. NOT AGAIN.

Saturday 6th May
I barely slept. The thought of another kid makes me mad. Once I've left home they can have as many babies as they like. But as long as I have to live in a noisy, smelly house, they need to wait. It's not fair.

I tried to distract myself with homework. It didn't work. If you want me to forget my worries, give me an ice cream or buy me a present. Forcing me to order decimals from smallest to largest won't take my mind off anything.

It was almost a relief when Mum popped her head round the door. 'We need a family meeting, Leez. Tomorrow, yeah?'

She doesn't look pregnant but it takes time.

Sunday 7<u>th</u> May

Well. I was not expecting that.

I'm not sure how to write about today. I'll let it settle overnight and see how I feel in the morning. Sorry, Auction Bidders, bear with me. All I'll say is, there's no new baby.

Monday 8<u>th</u> May

Sleeping on it hasn't helped. I'm still confused, but tired too. I must have looked troubled - isn't that a great word? It's exactly how I feel - because as soon as we sat on the bus, Jake said, 'What's up with your face?' Tbf, he's always saying that. I said, 'Sorry, I was thinking about something.' And he said, 'You OK? You don't seem yourself.' So I told him.

I told him that I've only ever had one grandparent - Grandma. That's because Mum's dad died when she was younger, and because Dad's parents don't speak to him. Ever since he got with Mum. They told him to stop seeing her, he refused, so they said he wasn't welcome in their house. He moved in with Mum, got married, and had all of us. No one's thought twice about the grandparents they've never known. And let's face it, Grandma's enough for anyone. Especially now she's added Will.

Jake said, 'Right,' really slowly. Like he had no idea where it was heading. By now we were nearly at school so I had to speed up.

'Dad got a letter from his mum. Out of the blue. She wants him to visit,' I said. 'Oh wow!' Jake said. 'Yeah, oh wow,' I carried on. 'He's not sure whether he should go. He says if he does, he wants us with him because we're his family. Mum said she'll go if Dad decides to, but she's not happy. She thinks they're stupid for pushing him away.'

Jake took it in. 'What's Mac going to do?' he said. I shrugged. 'He's asked us what we think. If we want to visit, he'll take us. If we aren't interested, he won't go himself. He's still angry.' Jake thought for a moment. 'I don't blame him. If my mum told me who I should go out with and threw me out if I didn't listen, I'd be fuming.' I laughed out loud. 'As if Cait would ever do that!' That's when it hit me. Telling your own child to get lost is massive. Poor Dad.

None of this makes it clearer. Do I want to meet my grandparents who've shown no interest in me for twelve years and who treated Dad and Mum badly? Putting it like that should make it simpler but it doesn't. Part of me is curious.

Tuesday 9th May
Sunday's family meeting was left open-ended. We're meeting again at the weekend to see what everyone thinks.

I tried to chat to Spike after school. He was watching TV with his shoes on the sofa. Mum would have told him to move but I wanted to get him onside. I sat next to him. He glared. 'What d'you want?' he said. I tried to act normal but I've never willingly sat next to Spike in my life. In the end, I gave up being subtle and just came out with it. 'What are you going to do about Dad's mum and dad. Do you want to meet them?' He didn't look up from the telly. 'Not bothered,' he said.

Some people might say that to cover their real feelings. When Spike said it, I believed him.

Wednesday 10th May
Mum and Dad were chattier today. She told him they were about to run out of teabags and he said, 'OK.' That's normal conversation, I suppose.

I guess it'll become clear at some point. A thunderbolt will strike me and I'll know exactly what to do. I hope it happens before Sunday. That's when we need to decide.

I came to bed early. Downstairs was still tense. I wanted to read my new book from English. It's called 'Gone' and it's sci-fi. That's not usually my thing but I'm intrigued. It's about a town where the adults disappear and the kids are left in charge. It might kick off in the story but I'd be well up for that in real life. At least I think I would. I'm sure there'd be downsides.

Thursday 11th May
It's like Ms. Phelps read my mind. She walked into class and her opening line was, 'You've just woken up

and every adult in your life has vanished. What do you do? How do you feel? What would happen at home, in your village, and in the world?'

We had to discuss in groups before feeding back to the class. It was interesting. Those with no younger brothers or sisters could only see the good stuff. James said he'd eat ice cream for dinner and there'd be no time limits on his phone. But Bella said she'd have to keep her sister fed and they might run out of food if there were no adults opening the shops.

Bella's only got one sister and she had loads of worries. Mum and Dad have really dropped me in it with my lot.

Friday 12th May

I keep thinking about something Ms. Phelps said. It's stuck in my head. As we were packing away our things, she said, 'Remember everyone, thought exercises like that are interesting. But the good news is, you're legally children.' Everyone groaned. No one feels like a child when they're in high school. She said, 'I know, I know, you're young people and it won't be long before you're adults. But no one needs to worry about the issues we've discussed. There are always grown-ups to talk to when things feel too much. None of us have gone anywhere.'

I think she'd panicked when Bella had been talking. Her stress about looking after her sister was huge. Not like James who could only see the upsides. I thought it was because he was an only child so couldn't imagine looking after anyone else. Then I remembered that so is Jake but he totally got it. He's spent way too much time round my house.

It was a quiet Friday Fooday. Everyone was thinking. (Except Spike. He never thinks.) Luckily that didn't stop Mum and Dad making macaroni cheese and garlic bread. The atmosphere may have been weird but the food was delish.

Saturday 13th May

It's a chilly afternoon. Everyone's in their rooms or sprawled on the couch. I'm supposed to be doing History but I've just reread Grandma's interview from March. I should do that more often seeing as how long it took to type out. There was a special word for that. (Transmitting? Transferring? Nope, I've forgotten.) The part where Grandma talked about having Mum was interesting. It makes me laugh because of how un-Grandma it sounds.

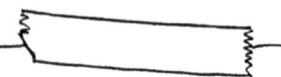

> GRANDMA: It's an odd feeling, Leeza. You've been through what can only be described as physical and mental hell. Then at the end, you're left with a tiny baby. And Molly was particularly tiny. Five pound four. And goodness me, she screamed the place down. At first I thought she didn't like me. I decided I was a terrible mother because my own child wouldn't stop screaming. But then a kind nurse told me that all babies scream. Of course, YOU know that, Leeza. So there we were, Molly and me. From her first breath I realised I couldn't make her do anything she didn't want to do. As she got older, I nagged her about the obvious things - tidying up and not staying out late. But I could never make her think or feel anything she didn't think or feel. She was her own person. And even though, as I'm sure you've learnt, that can be frustrating when you don't see eye to eye, it's also reassuring that your daughter does what she thinks is best. That's all you want for your children. That they do what they think is best and are happy with the consequences.
>
> (Will walks in.)
>
> WILL: How's the big interview? Is Ursula evading your questions? Shall I boo from the audience like Question Time.
> ME: Hi Will. She's doing good.
> GRANDMA: I'm doing well. Honestly Leeza. Your English is appalling. I blame your mother.
> WILL: Excellent. Right, back to my jam. Laters, Leez.
> (Will was making jam at the time.)

The Will part didn't need including. I just liked how all the details of Grandma's life were there. Thoughts about having a baby, next to her husband saying 'hi' and using up fruit from the garden.

And all the while, I was comparing it with Dad's situation. Perhaps I should have interviewed his parents. Maybe I'd understand them better. Or maybe they don't deserve my time. I wish my brain would tell me what to do. It's stopped working properly.

Ooh! Except the word I couldn't remember is 'transcribe'. My brain can work sometimes!

Sunday 14<u>th</u> May
Period – I completely forgot to count this month!

It's strange being asked my opinion about something big. Usually it's only small stuff. What film should we watch? What do you want for your birthday? Can you watch Harvest while I go to the loo? (That one happens way too much.) Being asked if you want to meet cruel grandparents is much bigger to decide.

The family meeting started slowly. Dad asked if we'd any thoughts and Spike jumped in with, 'I couldn't care less.' Dad kept a straight face and said, 'Thank you for your input, Spike. It's good to know where you stand.' Mum covered her mouth so no one could see her smile. (I spot everything!) Then Blane stood up and said, 'I will visit if you want.' He's getting way more confident. First, the christening comment last month, and now this. Well done Blane, I thought, as he sat down.

Mum looked at me. 'Well Leeza, what about you?' I shrugged. How could I say that I didn't know when I ALWAYS know? She said, 'It's not like you to be quiet. You must have an opinion.' Again, I shrugged because I couldn't find the words to explain.

Kenny was eating a biscuit so they didn't ask him, and Harvest was asleep in her chair. Dad looked around for a moment but no one else said anything. 'Looks like we're no further on. Would it help to have another week to think it over?'

That's when I snapped. Something shifted and it became clear. I leaned forward and let it out. 'NO, I don't think another week WOULD help. At least it wouldn't help ME. Because the past week has been RUBBISH. How are we supposed to know if we want to meet people we don't know? This is NOT something to put on your kids. This is up to YOU. You're the parents. You're the adults. We don't live in a world where big decisions are made by children because all the adults have vanished.' (They really need to read my book!) 'YOU have to decide if YOU want to see them again. And if you do, then THAT'S when you ask us to go. But you cannot force us to make an adult decision because you won't make it yourself.'

The breath I'd been holding in all week was out. PHEWWWWW. What a relief. But then I panicked. I'd shouted at Dad. Massively! I started to think how to backtrack but Mum stepped in. 'Leeza, thank goodness you're here. You're quite right. We wanted you involved but we forgot how much pressure that might be. It's an adult decision and one we'll have a think about. Thanks for being so mature.'

I thought she was being sarky but she ruffled my hair (get off!) and got up. Dad looked shocked but then clicked into action too. 'Well said, Leeza. Thank you. We'll let you know.' Then he went upstairs on his own.

Even though they're saying positive things, it feels like I went too far. What else could I do? Something tells me I won't sleep tonight.

Monday 15th May
I was right. Totally shattered.

Tuesday 16th May
In the olden days I'd have talked to Jenna. She was good at saying the right things to calm me down. FaceTiming isn't the same. She won't be able to work her magic online.

That left only one person. Jake. On the bus, James was showing him something on his phone. The rest of the day, there was no privacy and we didn't get a moment to ourselves.

School is like the McAuliffe household. No privacy, but less crying babies and more boring teachers.

Wednesday 17th May

I say 'boring teachers' but most of mine are OK. Especially Ms. Phelps. We're still reading 'Gone' in class. Even though it'd be bad for the adults to disappear, I think I'd cope on my own.

I wouldn't eat ice cream all day. I'd just enjoy having control over little things. Not big things like meeting Grandparents. Still no news on that front.

Thursday 18th May

Mum's been sucking up after my outburst. I thought I'd gone too far but she's acting like they did.

I was running late with a piece of toast in my mouth when she asked me. 'Is there anything you want for Friday Fooday seeing as it's your birthday weekend?' This is new. We get a birthday tea but it never stretches to weekends. I was taken aback.

Not so taken aback that I couldn't say 'baked goats cheese' between mouthfuls.

Friday 19th May
We hardly ever have baked goats cheese. Mum says it's too messy but I love it. You put a big wedge of cheese in a bowl, and add tomatoes, herbs, and garlic around the side. Then you bake it. That's it. When it comes out of the oven, it's boiling hot, the cheese is squishy, and the tomato sauce is gorge. Add bread for dipping and it's a great way to start the birthday celebrations.

Dad was cheerier this evening. He asked me what presents I wanted. It's in two days, so they've left it late. I said, 'You could let me have the house to myself for a day.' Mum snorted and Dad laughed. Then they carried on dipping their bread.

It was worth a shot.

Saturday 20th May
After breakfast, Mum said we were going shopping for my presents in the retail park. I didn't mind, although

I couldn't think of anything I'd want from there. There are clothes shops, a couple of coffee shops, a phone place, a big B&Q and the Tesco. There's also an Argos so I suppose that covers all sorts. Mum told us the plan first thing. But then it got interesting.

She said, 'It seems harsh to make you wait in the car. If you promise not to open the door, use the cooker, or break anything, you can stay here for a couple of hours.' YES, SHE REALLY SAID THAT.

I was properly gobsmacked (excellent word!) but I played it cool. Like an adult with my own demands, I said, 'Can I make a cup of tea?' 'One,' she said. 'Let's minimise the risks.' 'Can I have a bath?' I said. 'No. You might drown,' she answered. (I wouldn't.) 'The bathroom's for toilet time only, until we're back.' 'Can I invite my class over for a party?' I said. 'Aren't you hilarious,' she said. 'No chance.'

Next thing you know, everyone's getting their shoes on and being bundled into the car. Spike wasn't happy, but he had to go. I waved them off as they reversed out of the drive. It felt amazing.

I had no idea what to do with myself. It was so last-minute I had no plan. In the end, I did what I'd asked and made a cup of tea. Then I sat at the kitchen table and breathed deeply.

I didn't actually want a bath and I didn't care about inviting people over. But a cup of tea whilst I silently read my book was absolutely perfect. It was 2 hours and 37 minutes of complete happiness.

Yes, I counted every second.

Sunday 21st May
I'm 12!

I didn't think it could get any better but today was brilliant. It's not about presents. It's about attention. I felt special all day.

I never expect anything big. We've never had spare money and even though things are easier since we moved, we're not - as Grandma would say - Flash Harry. I don't know who Flash Harry is, but it's how she describes fancy people. (She's the fanciest person I know! She should be called Flash Harriet.)

Mum and Dad put my presents at the end of the bed for when I woke up. Mum shouted across the landing, 'Don't get excited. It's just bits.' I like bits so that was fine.

I got a hardbacked notebook, some eye liner and mascara, fairy lights for my room, and a heart shaped cushion for my bed. I like how they know me well. Fairy lights are my absolute favourite type of lights. They should be in every room.

Then Dad brought me breakfast in bed, saying, 'Don't get used to it.' I snuggled on my cushion and read the fairy light instructions as I ate my toast. I'm going to hang them across the curtain rail.

The rest of the day's going to be busy. Grandma and Will are coming for tea and we're going to - DRUM ROLL PLEASE - the pub! Yes, I've requested a pub meal for my birthday. Spike was allowed one last year so they can't refuse.

Auction Bidders, enjoy the rest of your day. I know I will.

<u>Monday 22nd May</u>
OMG. Grandma got me a phone!!!!!!!!!

I CANNOT believe it. It was the BIGGEST surprise and Mum and Dad already knew! The three of them planned it ages ago. Grandma told them all her friends' grandkids have phones and as I get a school bus, I should have one too. AND THEY AGREED. I spent all last night setting it up. It's the BEST.

I've used the 'all the other kids have one' line many times. It's never worked. Grandma is a witch. A really GOOD witch.

<u>Tuesday 23rd May</u>
I've spent all day playing on my phone. Time flies when you've got YouTube at your fingertips. There are rules, obvs. Homework has to be done before screen time, I can't use it when we're eating, and Mum and Dad have to approve any apps. I'll take that, no worries.

I still can't believe it. An actual phone. I'm so lucky.

Wednesday 24th May

Jake asked me about Dad in registration. 'Has Mac decided what to do about his mum's letter?'

It shows how preoccupied I've been. I'd forgotten all about that since my phone. I said, 'No, he's still thinking. It's not been mentioned since.'

Jake said, 'Aren't you curious? You've got their genes. Don't you want to see what they're like?' I understood what he meant. Mainly because we've been doing genes in Science. Also, I AM curious. I don't think I'll be like them but Dad might be. It's hard to imagine. He was a fully grown adult when he met Mum. I'm nosy about the people that started him off.

I was still thinking about that when Jake said, 'If my dad ever got in touch, I'd want to know what he's like. I wouldn't be friends with him but I'd want to see what bits he passed on to me.'

I hadn't thought about that. Jake's dad has never come up before. Now I'm nosy about what he's like.

Maybe I'm nosy about anyone's family.

Thursday 25th May

The message in today's assembly was, 'Treat other people the way you'd want to be treated yourself.' It's not new, is it? That's been said at assemblies since I was four. Except today was different. I kept thinking about Dad's parents. They pushed him away and now they want him to visit. They didn't treat him the way they wanted to be treated themselves.

Friday 26th May

Break up for half term.

Tom had pasta going out of date so Mum invited him, Cait, and Jake over. (There was loads to eat before midnight.) That's how I ended up with Jake, hanging fairy lights on my curtain rail, and feeling so full I might burst.

He was handy because he's tall. He's the tallest boy in Class 1. I had him twisting the wire around the pole so that I could still open and close the curtains. That's trickier than it sounds but we managed it.

When it was done, we switched off the main light. With pillows under our heads, we lay on the floor, with our legs resting on the bed. The lights looked amazing. If I wasn't so full of pasta, I'd have felt amazing too.

Jake was quiet. He'd done a lot of stretching. Or maybe he was full as well. In the end I said, 'You OK?' He turned to look at me. His face was serious. 'I think you should meet your grandparents.' That surprised me. I didn't know what to say so he carried on. 'If I had the chance to meet my dad, I definitely would. I've been thinking about it for ages. Since that stupid book in English. I've got Mum and I've got Grandad, but that's it. That's not many people. D'you know the royal family never get on the same plane in case it crashes and everyone's wiped out? Mum and Grandad get in the same car all the time. I'd have no one. In a few years, all your lot will be grown up and you'll be mates.

You'll probably have loads of people around you. But just in case you don't, you should definitely meet your grandparents. You never know, you might need them.'

I wanted to make a joke about how I'll never be mates with Spike. Or how there's no way my parents could afford to take everyone on a plane that might wipe them out. But I stayed quiet. Instead, I reached across and held Jake's hand. I wanted to show that I cared.

Sometimes that's all you can do, isn't it?

Saturday 27th May

I woke up at 8.49 but stayed in bed until 11.35. Now I've got my phone, I always know the time. It wasn't all lazing around though. I was thinking. It's Jake's fault. He put lots of thoughts into my head. And because it's Jake, I have to pay attention to them.

So yeah, lots to think about today.

Sunday 28th May

I keep getting texts from Grandma. My first message said COME IN LEEZA MCAULIFFE, ARE YOU

READING ME? OVER. It was only a few hours after I'd opened my phone and it was still charging. She sent it while she was sitting opposite me, then laughed to herself until I read it.

Today's message was TELL YOUR MOTHER TO STOP IGNORING MY TEXTS. I've no idea if Mum is ignoring her texts, except she usually does. I hope I'm not going to be used as a family messenger. I don't need the hassle.

Monday 29th May
I finished 'Gone'. It threw up some big ideas. I think it's doubly clever to write something like that. It's good to read but it makes you ponder stuff too. I can't stop thinking about how Jake's feeling. I've never had to worry about him before.

Tuesday 30th May
Mum spent breakfast going through the iPad and deleting the blurry pictures. (All taken by Blane) But later, when I was in my room, she knocked and handed me a bunch of printed photos from my birthday.

There's some from the pub and a few from Friday Fooday with Jake. That's what gave me the idea.

I ditched my homework and started to plan. It took me an hour and I had to root in the drawer for the glue and scissors. It's not the best, but it's something. I'll take it down to Jake's tomorrow.

Wednesday 31st May
I walked down the lane after dinner. When Mum heard I was going, she sent me with a list for the shop. I don't like being used but I took a bag and put Jake's present in it.

I had to explain it to him. 'It's a collage of all the people in your life,' I said. He looked at it and started to smile. I'd cut out photos of Tom and Cait, but I'd added Mum, Dad, Me, Spike, Blane, Kenny, Harvest, Grandma, and Will. I'd even added extra people from the pub that were in the background. 'There's not a car big enough to wipe out this lot. You've got people. You've got me.' He took the card and kept smiling. I finished with, 'Worst case scenario, if most of us are squashed by a meteorite, you'll have to move in with my grandma. But Will can keep you sane.'

That's when Jake's eyes started to water. I could see them shining through his hair. He was still smiling as he wiped them with his sleeve. 'That's the best thing ever,' he said. And then we hugged. Tight. I've never hugged Jake before. We've wrestled and pretended to fight, but this was different.

When I got home, Mum and Dad were in the kitchen feeding mush to Harvest. I put the shopping on the table and turned to Dad. 'If you want me to visit your parents, I will. I don't mind. It might be interesting.'

He nodded, said thank you, then wiped away Harvest's orange puke. An everyday event which made things seem normal. Even if they weren't.

6

Family Dramas – Plural

<u>Thursday 1st June</u>

I should write a story called The Last-Minute Homework Monster. He comes at the end of every school holiday whether I like it or not.

That's a great idea for a horror story, btw. I have great ideas when I'm allowed to think for myself. Instead, I was stuck with simplifying fractions, labelling electrical circuits, and reading about the rock cycle. I'm sure whoever thought up those topics was pleased with themselves, but my Last-Minute Monster is well better.

<u>Friday 2nd June</u>
Homework all day. Booo!

Veggie kebabs and flatbread for tea. Yay!

Saturday 3rd June
Dad spent the morning upstairs. I asked Mum what he was doing and she said, 'Writing to his mum. He'll be a while.' I suppose it's hard to find the words.

When he came down, he walked straight over to Mum, kissed her neck (she was feeding Harvest) and said, 'Come on Blane, let's nail that bike riding.'

Blane and his stabilisers have been stressing him for ages. Blane's not bothered but Dad thinks it's his job to teach him. Even I can see it's not worth the hassle.

Sunday 4th June
End of holiday blues all day. Life will be so much better when no one is telling me where to be from 9.15am to 3.15pm every day. FACT.

Monday 5th June
Back to school.

I've not seen Jake since the collage but we've had loads of messages. My last one was I THOUGHT ABOUT IT AND I TOLD MY DAD I'LL GO. His reply was GR8 LEEZ. I'M HERE IF YOU WANNA TALK ABOUT IT. I know he's there. He's always there. But to know 'he's there' is comforting.

The BIG news of the day (sarcasm!) is that Blane rode his bike by himself. For ten seconds. We stood on the lane as Dad ran behind him. When he climbed off, Dad lifted him onto his shoulders and we all cheered. It was sweet. Blane smiled through his shyness and Dad felt a sense of achievement.

Then we went back inside and got on with the evening.

Tuesday 6th June

There's been no rain for over a week. That means we can leave the garden chairs out overnight. We used to do that in Stockford but they were filthy and no one liked sitting on them. Since we moved to Applemere, we've been better at keeping them clean.

Because of that, we ate tea outside. Outside teas might be my absolute favourite, even when they're salad. (Tonight's was salad.)

Wednesday 7<u>th June</u>
Poppy stared at me. For no reason. As we waited to go into English, she pulled a face for way too long. When I stared back, she said, 'Who d'ya think you're looking at?' which was daft because she started it. Then Ms. Phelps arrived and it was over. Once again Jake wasn't there. He was running late to class and turned up as we were sitting down.

With that drama over, I thought the rest of the day would be calm. But no. It all kicked off at home. I didn't see it happen. We'd finished eating but I was drinking my juice at the table. Spike had gone outside to check his potatoes and everyone else was doing their own thing.

Suddenly there was a massive scream. I looked at the back door and Blane was there, holding his hand.

There was blood.

I'm not sure if I've told you this, Auction Bidders, but I can't stand blood. As soon as I saw it, I knew I wasn't the person to take charge. I shouted for Mum and Dad. Obvs shouting was pointless as they'd heard Blane too. They came running in and immediately took over. They picked him up, got a towel to clean his hand, and looked at how bad it was. From the look on their faces, it was BAD.

Next thing, Mum's on the phone to Cait, Dad's getting the postcode of the A and E, (a lot further away than the one in Stockford) and instructions are being shouted all over the place.

Ten minutes later, Tom and Cait arrived. Tom took the rest of us into the living room while Cait had a look at Blane's hand. It was his middle finger. He'd followed Spike outside but the door slammed shut on it. Mum used her fake-cheerful voice which means there's defo nothing to be cheerful about. I see through all her voices.

Blane had calmed down but was still whimpering. Cait stuck butterfly stitches onto his finger (Mum said later, it had been 'hanging off.' **Urggghhh!**) but she thought he'd need proper stitches to heal better. Mum, Dad, and Blane went to the hospital around 8 o'clock. Cait went back home to Jake and Tom stayed with us. It's 10.30pm, I've come up to bed and Tom's still downstairs. I hope Blane's OK.

Thursday 8<u>th</u> June
If I hadn't remembered in time, it would've been a huge shock to find Tom snoring on the sofa. That's what happened this morning. I walked into the living room and there he was.

I panicked. If he was still here, that must mean Blane was not. He must have been rushed into theatre for life-saving surgery. What if it went wrong? What if his hand was mangled forever? How would he cope? He'd only just learnt how to ride his bike.

Then Mum came up behind me. 'Shhh, let him sleep. Your toast's over there.' I looked towards the kitchen and there was Blane! Sitting down, eating a jam sandwich, and resting his bandaged hand on the table. I've never felt so relieved.

'We got back a few of hours ago...' Mum said, '...but Tom was already asleep. It seemed best to leave him after all his help.' I looked at Blane, trying to imagine how scared he must have been. 'I got stickers,' he said, as he licked jam from his mouth.

Friday 9th June
Jake's been funny the last couple of days. He keeps calling Tom a dirty stop out. Last time he was out all night, he was playing poker with Billy.

Everyone's worn out. Dad said it was because we'd been stressed about Blane and had lots of adrenaline. Now it's dropped away, our bodies feel tired. I forget Dad knows things. I asked him more questions about adrenaline and he gave me stuff to look up. I think I've found an interesting side to biology.

Saturday 10th June
I've been online all day. Learning about how our bodies react to stress. There's a thing called 'fight, flight, faint, or freeze.' It's from the olden days - when cavewomen and cavemen were alive. If something threatened them, like a dinosaur or a baddie, then their

brain would sense the danger and react. It might 'fight' and stand up to the scary thing. It might take 'flight' or run away to somewhere safe. It might 'faint' which is exactly what it says, or it might 'freeze' and be unable to move or do anything.

When Blane cut his finger, I think I froze. That's better than fainting which would have been my next choice. When Poppy stared at me in the corridor, I think I fought. I stood my ground and stared back.

I don't seem to fly away. I stick around even when I don't do anything. Interesting.

Sunday 11<u>th</u> June
I got it wrong. I thought it was Biology that I'd been reading about but Dad said it was Psychology. When I asked what the difference was, he shrugged and said, 'Psychology's the interesting one.' That didn't answer my question.

Jake knocked this afternoon. He had a present for Blane. 'Grandad said to give you these,' as he handed over three jars of jam. Blane looked like he was bursting with happiness. He took them from Jake one at a time and put them on the kitchen top. Then when Jake held out his hand for a high-five, Blane smacked it really hard. He's defo growing in confidence these days.

Blane, not Jake.

Monday 12th June

'Any more family drama?' Jake asked as I arrived at the bus stop. 'Nah, all done,' I said. Which is the stupidest thing to say. There's always more drama.

When I got in, Mum was boiling the kettle. 'Tea break,' she said, and smiled. I smiled back even though she didn't have to explain. Then she said, 'Will you have much homework this weekend?' 'Same as usual probably,' I said, and kicked off my shoes. She was quiet for a minute - busy fishing out tea bags and sorting the milk. Then, with a cup in each hand, she walked past me and stopped at the bottom of the stairs. 'Get as much done as you can on Friday. Your dad's mum's been on. We're seeing them in Manchester on Saturday.'

I nodded and she went back up. It was a perfectly ordinary thing to say but it felt weird as anything.

Tuesday 13th June
Everything is mixed up and blurry. I'm not sure why. Seeing my unknown grandparents could be nice. (It could also be terrible, but for now, I'm being positive.) Mum seems OK, Dad hasn't said much, and everyone else is being themselves.

At lunch I was scrolling through my messages and saw Jake's from last week. When he said he was 'there' for me. It was nice to remember. Today, however, he was fake-fighting with James on the bus, sitting on the other side of the room in the lessons we had together, and listening to music on the way home. I waved at him as I walked down the lane.

It was a very Jake-free day. I'll fill him in another time.

Wednesday 14th June
I've got stomach ache again. The butterflies are going mad. My body knows it's going to be experiencing

something weird in a few days. I wonder what my other grandma looks like?

Thursday 15th June

I asked Mum what my other grandma looks like. 'No idea these days,' she said. 'Back then, just normal.' I sighed. What does that even mean? Mum must have heard because she had another go. 'She had brown hair and was about my height. And she wore normal clothes.' That time I rolled my eyes. Mum clocked it, so she had one more try. 'What I mean is, she wore stuff that didn't stand out from the crowd. Tops and trousers, or a skirt and jumper. Nothing like my mum, is what I mean.'

I understood then. 'Normal clothes' meant normal clothes. My stranger-grandma was like everyone else's grandma. Not like my real grandma who once spent the same amount on a winter coat as our family spends on a month of food shopping. (A fact that came up during one of Mum and Grandma's rows.)

Even though the coat story makes her sound ridiculous, I don't want Stranger-Grandma to be better than Real-Grandma. What if she's more fun? Or less obsessed with tidying? On paper, Real-Grandma has quite a few negative qualities.

Friday 16th June
Period. That's all I need.

I'm not sure whether the butterflies were period pains or worries about what's going on. It's no fun second guessing myself.

I think Mum and Dad are nervous too. They used Family Fooday like a family meeting. After we'd filled our plates (veggie chilli and potato wedges) Dad said, 'I thought now might be a good time to answer any questions you've got about tomorrow.' Spike jumped in straight away. 'Can we drive down Tyson Road?' Dad nodded. 'If there's time.' Then Blane piped up. 'What are the people called?' I thought it was sweet he'd asked a question even if we already knew their names. Then it hit me. I have no idea what they're called. I keep calling Dad's mum, 'Stranger-Grandma', and I've given his dad no thought at all. My brain isn't used to grandads.

Dad said, 'What a good question Blane. My dad's called Dougie and my mum's called Jeanette. He was quiet for a moment. Mum touched his hand and said, 'Maybe you could tell us what they were like?' She knows exactly what they were like, but she was thinking of us. I nodded and so did Blane. Spike carried on eating his wedges but kept looking up, so I guess he was interested too.

Dad sighed and said, 'Right, let's think. I suppose they always had strong views about things.' 'Like Grandma!' I said. Dad laughed. 'Not quite like Grandma.' He smiled for a second before carrying on. 'Grandma has strong views, for sure. But we laugh them off when we don't agree. Sometimes your mum has a go, but it blows over and we carry on. My parents weren't like that.' He paused again, like he didn't know how to explain. 'They were harder to get along with. We were never close.'

Mum could see it wasn't easy for him to find the right words. She jumped in. 'Tomorrow will be interesting however it plays out. You'll meet people you're related to, and maybe Dad'll find his parents easier, now they've had a break for a few years.'

Then the chat was over and it was a normal Friday night. Dad played music, and we chatted about school stuff, Kenny's writing, and Spike's potatoes. By the time I came to bed I'd almost forgotten how strange tomorrow will be. Almost but not quite.

Saturday 17th June

We've just got back and I'm too tired to write. Also, I don't know what to say. I need to sleep on it. One thing I do know... it was odd going past 620 Tyson Road. It looks the same but feels different. Also, when I lived there, I'd never met my stranger-grandma. And as of today, I certainly have.

Sunday 18th June

I woke up to a message from Jake. HOW DID IT GO? MSG ME. I smiled as I rolled out of bed. That shows I'm not too freaked out. Nothing bad happened. Not really. The whole day just felt... I don't know. I got dressed and asked Mum if I could go down to Jake's.

She said, 'Absolutely…' she was changing Harvest's nappy, '…but take this list. Here's my card.'

Cait let me in on her way out, Tom said hello before going to open the shop, and Jake got me a juice. He was wearing a hairband. 'Like Jack Grealish,' he said. I know he's a footballer but I can't picture him. Anyway, I can see Jake's face now. I'd forgotten how smiley his eyes are.

Finally, we were alone. 'Right,' he said. 'How was it?' I'd been thinking about that all night. All I could come up with was the old classic - WEIRD. 'Ms. Phelps would tell you to use a different word,' Jake said. I knew that, but I couldn't think of one. 'Start at the beginning,' he said. 'But only if you want to.' I definitely wanted to. Who else could I talk to?

I took a swig of juice and began. 'We got up early. Mum made us be extra smart and ironed. We were wearing our Christmas clothes, which was a mistake because we were boiling.' 'Good plan, Molly!' Jake laughed. 'Go on.'

I thought about what parts to tell him. Whether I needed to explain how weird it was to go past my old house with its new door. Or how jealous I felt of everyone getting the bus into town. Like we used to do. I'm not sure he'd have got that part. I skipped ahead to the actual visit.

'We pulled up outside. It was the house my dad grew up in, but it looked like no one lived there. I don't mean scruffy or falling down. I mean it was blank and empty. But we knocked, and the door opened, and my other grandma was standing there.' I stopped for more juice before carrying on. 'She looked down at us and said, 'Well look at all of you.' And then she looked at Dad and said, 'Seb. Thank you for coming.' And then she looked at Mum and said, 'Molly, you look exactly the same.' And her mouth was smiling but her eyes were sad. We followed inside and she told us to have a seat, but she spent ages moving cushions and fussing. Dad was being polite and asked how she was. And even as I'm saying this, it doesn't sound strange, but it was. No one was real. No one was silly or jokey. It was like the first day with a new teacher, when you don't know how much of a laugh they'll be.' I had another swig. My throat was dry. 'After a few dining chairs were brought in, we had a seat. Then she went to the kitchen and brought out a plate of biscuits and put the kettle on. But Kenny tripped up on his way to the coffee table so he started crying. And then Harvest had a whinge because she'd just woken up. And Mum was trying to get everyone to be quiet whilst Dad went to see if his mum needed help because, as he said, it's not easy to rustle up a tray of juice and a pot of tea when you're only used to two of you.'

Jake was an excellent listener. He just let me pour it out. When I finished, he asked, 'And what about your grandad?' I shook my head. It was the weirdest thing of all.

'We didn't see him,' I said.

Monday 19th June
I finished telling Jake but I couldn't be bothered writing everything last night. The short story is that Jeanette had decided enough was enough. While Dad's dad was at a hospital appointment, she'd arranged for us to visit. She'd wanted to do it for ages but Dad's dad

had always stopped her. When I heard that, I liked her more. I also felt sorry for her.

We stayed for a couple of hours and left before he was due back. At first I worried Jeanette might be in danger. That if Dad's dad found out we'd been there, he might beat her up, or something bad like that. That's what happened to the woman who lived four doors down in Stockford. One day her horrible husband was taken away by the police and it all came out. But I don't think that's how it is with Jeanette. As we were leaving, her eyes were smiling as well as her mouth. She said to Dad, 'You remember what he's like. He needs to come round to an idea in his own time. I'll work on him.'

That's exactly how Real-Grandma made Will ditch his patterned jumpers.

Tuesday 20th June
Blane is 7!

It was a rush but Blane managed to open his presents (his finger is still sore) and have pain au chocolat before school. (He asked for chocolate bread but I know the proper name.) He got paints, books, new shorts, and a slime making kit. Spike looked well jealous.

For tea we had pizza! We all remember when he chose jam sandwiches last year. I'd been worried we might be in for something similar, but no. He'd chosen pizza and I was well happy. My favourite topping? Cheese, extra cheese, and a bit more cheese on top, thank you.

Blane's also been made cloakroom monitor. He's had the best day.

Wednesday 21st June

Dad got a letter from his mum. He read it out while we were eating. I can't remember it exactly but she said it was lovely to see us. Dad finished reading and said, 'Me and your mum are very proud. You were perfectly behaved and showed what a fantastic team we are.' Mum got up and patted his shoulder while he sniffed a couple of times. I think he was sad and happy at the same time. Sad because his mum went along with his dad for so long, but happy that he'd seen her again.

It was Spike who asked the question. 'Why did she want to see you now?' I don't get that either. Her first letter was out of the blue. 'No idea,' Dad said, and shrugged. Mum said, 'Sometimes it can take a long time to find the strength to stand up for yourself. It's nice that Grandma Jeanette came round eventually.'

All of this has thrown up lots to think about. First off, I'm not sure Grandma Jeanette is what I want to call Dad's mum. I know I need something better than Stranger-Grandma but I've not decided yet. Secondly, the thought of calling Real-Grandma, Grandma Ursula, makes me lol. She'd HATE it. I might try it next time I see her.

Thursday 22nd June
Big gossip from school - sarcasm! James and Lexi have split up. I was washing my hands in the toilets when Lexi and Poppy came in. Poppy said things like, 'You're better than him,' and, 'He didn't realise how lucky he was to have you.' They ignored me (good) and I left before I heard any more gossip.

Jake filled me in later. Apparently, James and Lexi had been seeing each other since February. I hadn't realised it'd been that long. According to Jake, James got fed up of being told what to wear. I burst out laughing when I heard that. Lexi wears full makeup and rolls up her blazer sleeves to look cool. (And she does!) But James is just a boy in a uniform. I wonder what sort of make-over Lexi was pushing.

'Careful,' I said, as I got off the bus. 'You might be next on Lexi's list. She'll be making you bin your grey joggers.' Jake laughed as we went our separate ways. 'Not my type,' he shouted back.

Now all I can think is, what IS Jake's type? And whoever they are, will they put up with me hanging around?

Friday 23rd June
So far this year, I've had to deal with strange relatives, Poppy's rudeness, and feeling icky about Jake getting a girlfriend. And he hasn't even got a girlfriend. As far as I know.

In January, all I was worried about was what my 'New Year, New You' was going to be. I still haven't given up finding my unique qualities. There must be some things that only I can do, say, or think. And when I know what they are, I can change them. My 'New Year, New You' will just be a little later than everyone else.

Maybe I'll be ready for next January.

Saturday 24th June
I was having a lie in when a piece of paper was pushed under the door. In shaky handwriting, it said...

> To Leeza
> Famlee meeting toomow in the kichen.
> From Blane
> x

I got back into bed, thinking how cute Blane could be, and wondering what on earth he wanted to talk about.

Sunday 25th June
The good news is, the family meeting didn't involve a huge announcement or any stressful drama. I knew it

wouldn't because Blane called it, but there's always that worry.

Dinner was running late, so the pans were boiling when it was time to start. No one said anything. Mum kept one eye on the hob and Blane sat waiting like the rest of us. Eventually Dad said, 'Well Blane, here we are. Thank you for inviting us to your meeting. What would you like to talk about?'

For a shy kid, it must have been scary. All eyes were on him and he looked terrified. He took a few big swallows and looked around. In the tiniest voice ever he said, 'From now on, we need to keep our coats tidy.'

Spike burst out laughing until Mum shot him daggers. I managed to control myself. (It WAS funny.) Dad was the one who took charge. 'What an excellent idea. Do you think we've let things slip?' Blane nodded. Dad said, 'How about after the meeting, we go to the hooks and make sure everything's hanging up properly.' Blane nodded again. He'd used up all his bravery. Dad said, 'Is there anything you can suggest, so we're tidier? What have you been doing in school?' Blane's eyes went wide as he realised he'd have to speak again. Eventually he whispered, 'I check the cloakroom and tell Miss if it's messy.'

By now Spike's attention had gone. Kenny hadn't been listening anyway, and Harvest was busy sucking her bottle. Mum got up to turn down the hob, so it was left to me to represent the family, and not leave it all to Dad. 'What do you want me to do, Blane?' I asked.

Suddenly his bravery came back and his voice was loud and firm. 'Hang your coat up, Leeza,' he said.

Monday 26th June

Dad's given Blane a notebook so he can write down when the coats fall off the hooks. Spike was fuming. He said, 'This is messed up,' as he left for school. As the door shut, I heard Dad say, 'It's so he can practise his writing. It's not really about the coats, mate.'

Spike will not be convinced that easily.

Tuesday 27th June

Once again, Jake knows my family news as soon as it's happened. 'I hope you remembered to HANG YOUR COAT UP, LEEZA,' is what he said when I got to the bus stop. My face must have looked baffled (great word!) 'Molly was on the phone with Mum last night. She kept doing an impression of Blane. I could hear it across the room.' 'Great,' I said. 'Nice to know my ridiculous family entertains you.'

The bus came so the conversation moved on. 'How're the fairy lights?' he said. 'The best thing about my room,' I said. 'How's the rest of the family?' he added. 'Not bad,' I said. 'Harvest's pulling herself up to the furniture now.' 'No way!' he said. 'It's hardly any time since that night.'

It wasn't a massive conversation. Just a comfortable one. I like how Jake only needs to say 'that night' and we both know what he means. (Her birth, Auction Bidders! I've just looked back at last year's diary to remind myself. It was the most stressful Harvest Festival in history!) I've known Jake less than a year but it's like we've got our own secret language. We know what we mean, even when we don't explain properly.

(Wow, McAuliffe! Stop being ridic about secret language rubbish. Get. A. Grip.)

Wednesday 28th June
I should tell myself to get a grip more often. I had a great night's sleep. Next time my mind's running away with itself, I'll give it a talking to, and snap back to normal. Whatever normal is.

Kenny wrote his name all the way through for the first time. He's been close for ages but today he got both Ns right. Mum told him to take a victory lap and show everyone. I was getting changed into my PJs when he walked in. I was mostly done so it was fine. I said, 'Nice one Kenny!' which seemed enough. Then he wandered off to find the next person. Spike was in the loo so Kenny sat outside the door until he came out.

I'm not sure Spike's thumbs up when he finally finished was worth it.

Thursday 29th June

Speaking of family achievements, Spike's potatoes are ready to eat. I never thought they'd come to anything but I was wrong. Spike announced the news at breakfast. As he climbed onto his chair, Mum panicked. 'Do it from your seat, Spike, for the love of God.' He ignored her and milked the attention. 'I am pleased to tell you that today, for the first time, we have real live potatoes! They will be cooked, eaten, and will taste amazing. They will be the best potatoes you've ever seen and your tummies will be happy that you knew Spike McAuliffe, gardening master and brilliantest potato expert.'

I clapped along with everyone else. If there's ever a national shortage of crisps, there are worse people to live with.

Friday 30th June

Everyone's achieving things atm. Harvest's really close to stepping along the couch. Kenny's writing is getting better and better. Blane is the coat monitor of the house and Spike has dug up his potatoes. (We had them boiled with salt and butter. Actually delish. For real.)

We're half way through the year and everyone's getting on with their lives. I can already walk, my writing's good, I can call a meeting if I want, and if I did grow potatoes they'd be tasty too. I know I can do everything my brothers and sisters can do. But I'm struggling to do my *own* things. I never have any announcements. School's fine. I can usually do the work but I'm not top of the class. That's OK because I don't need to be. But it'd be nice to know what I AM good at.

Because at the back of my mind, there's the worrying thought, that maybe I'm good at nothing. Nothing at all.

7

Wingspreading

<u>Saturday 1st July</u>

I woke up to hear Mum shout, 'It's Saturday morning, the sun's shining, and you're missing a beautiful day.' I rolled over and had another hour.

It's like she doesn't even know me.

<u>Sunday 2nd July</u>

Yesterday WAS a beautiful day. If you like hot sun and nothing to do, that is. It was the same today. I had my lunch with Harvest outside on a blanket. (She had a rusk, I had a cheese and cucumber sandwich.) It was OK for a while. We sat in the shade and watched Spike water the soil. I don't like the gunky feeling of Mum's factor 50 so I stayed out of the sun. It's clear I'm an indoors person.

Having said that, the BBQ for tea was brilliant. I didn't mind being outside for that.

Monday 3<u>rd</u> July
The first thing Jake said when we sat down was, 'Looking forward to our last month together?' I looked blank. 'Y7 and Y8 are Class 1,' he said. 'Y9 and Y10 are Class 2. In September we'll be in different rooms. How will you cope?' I got it. He was joking about how hard it'll be in class without him.

Except it's true. Who else am I proper friends with? No one. That's who. September's going to be strange.

Tuesday 4<u>th</u> July
While Miss Wilkinson was telling us about Sports Day, I looked around the room. Is there a potential best friend amongst the class? There are 15 people in Class 1 but there are some Y8s I've never spoken to. There's no point now. In September they'll be off to Class 2 with Jake.

The only good thing is that Poppy will also be moving up. But what if that pushes her and Jake together? Agghhhh.

I think, over the coming weeks, I'll be writing more screams than usual.

<u>Wednesday 5th July</u>
This morning a letter arrived from Spike and Blane's school. Kenny's starting Reception in September and his class teacher is doing a home visit.

This isn't a big deal. All of us had home visits when we were little. I was off sick when Mrs. Ali visited Blane. It was funny seeing the Reception teacher in my living room. In a nice way. Defo nothing to stress over.

Tell that to Mum. She let out a massive groan. 'Mac, the school are coming!' Dad was calmer. He finished his mouthful of cereal and said, 'Great,' in a sarcastic way.

When I got in from school, there was a note on the fridge next to a new behaviour chart for Spike. FROM NOW UNTIL MONDAY, THIS HOUSE REMAINS

SPOTLESS. WASH UP YOUR DISHES. PICK UP YOUR CLOTHES FROM THE FLOOR. DO NOT LET HARVEST NEAR CRAYONS.

Mum saw me reading it while I swigged milk from the carton. She'd been wiping the window sills and had come to rinse the cloth. 'Don't you think you're overreacting?' I said. 'Irwell Green did home visits and you weren't like this.'

Mum squeezed out the cloth and turned to face me. 'Irwell Green got to know our family through you. You started school first and gave them a positive impression of us. The home visits that followed were a doddle.' She looked around in case anyone was listening before lowering her voice to a whisper. 'Spike is the first McAuliffe kid that place has met. Last week they rang to say he'd pushed a kid's face into their beetroot cake.' (That explains the behaviour chart.) 'This visit has to undo all the negative press he's given us. God help Kenny on his first day if they think they're getting another Spike.' She knew she'd said too much. She dried her hands and tried to smile. 'Just keep things clean, yeah?'

So one of my talents is providing good press for the McAuliffes? Not what I was hoping for, but it's a start.

Thursday 6th July

Grandma was coming up on Saturday but Mum's rescheduled because of the home visit. Putting on a show is right up Grandma's street. Her house was always spotless even when we'd turn up without warning. How does that happen? She must clean even when she's NOT expecting visitors.

She texted me this evening. LEEZA, I WON'T SEE YOU THIS WEEKEND SO REMIND YOUR MOTHER THAT DUST SETTLES EVERYWHERE. I messaged back. WHY DON'T YOU MESSAGE HER YOURSELF?

Ages later I got a reply. SHE IGNORES MY MESSAGES. I laughed to myself because she was right. Sort of. She reads them but doesn't reply. I was still thinking about that when she messaged again. WILL MADE ME GO TO A CAR BOOT SO I BOUGHT YOU A BOOK. I'LL POP IT IN THE POST TOMORROW. I was tired so I thought I'd end the conversation the only way I knew how. THANK YOU. CAN I CALL YOU GRANDMA URSULA FROM NOW ON?

She didn't take ages that time. NOT IF YOU WANT TO LIVE she messaged. I laughed to myself as I got ready for bed.

Friday 7th July

Funny how things change. Miss Wilkinson gave out next week's test timetable and here's the thing... I didn't think twice about it. But for the whole of Y6, Ms. Archer went on about the SATs like they were the biggest deal ever. I prefer the Applemere Bridge way of doing it. No one cares. They're just tests.

Friday Fooday was BBQed veggie burgers, BBQed jacket wedges, and BBQed courgettes. If I've not been clear, we had a BBQ.

Saturday 8th July

The good thing about this time of year is that teachers keep forgetting to set homework. Today was a lovely, chilled, contented sort of day. I felt like a lazy cat purring in the sun.

My lack of homework was great but the book from Grandma has arrived. It looks just as dull as homework. It's called 'Little Women' and it's from years ago. Even longer ago than Enid Blyton. Her note said, 'Every girl should read this,' which sent Mum into a rant. She said, 'Every girl should do what they want and not behave exactly the same as each other.' She was quiet for a moment before adding, 'Having said that, I did enjoy 'Little Women' when I was younger.'

It's hard to keep up with the mixed messages at times.

Sunday 9th July

It couldn't last. Today, instead of a lazy cat, I was a hard-working, non-stop, busy little... I'm trying to think of an animal that's made to clean windows and brush soil off the patio... no I can't think of one, but that's what I was. We'll all be glad when tomorrow's over and Kenny has met his teacher.

Kenny, btw, doesn't care about any of this. It's probably best.

Monday 10th July

Even though these tests aren't as bad as last year's, they're still tests. We didn't have to separate our desks and the rules weren't as strict, but today was no fun. I was glad to go home.

I never thought I'd enjoy the noise levels in the house until I'd sat in silence all day. Even Spike shouting that he'd run out of loo roll was more entertaining than usual.

The big news is that Kenny's home visit is over. His teacher and teaching assistant came this afternoon and Mum and Dad managed to be normal for half an hour. Mum said, 'I channelled your Grandma and pretended that Kenny has a calm, and uneventful home life.' 'Shouldn't you always be yourself, no matter what?' I said. She didn't hear me. She wasn't done thinking about the visit. 'We were home free until Mrs. Winn clocked Spike's behaviour chart. I don't need patronising from a woman that gets paid to do what I do for free.' My last comment must have sunk in. She looked at me for a moment and said, 'We can be ourselves now that we're back on track with the school.'

She does talk rubbish sometimes.

Tuesday 11th July
More tests. Boring.

Wednesday 12th July
Mum said something funny this morning. Funny weird, not funny joking. She was asking how school was going and said, 'I don't need to worry about you. You take everything in your stride.' I didn't know what that meant. She said, 'Some people get nervous before tests. They don't sleep the night before and worry they won't remember anything. You just get on with them. It's a good thing.'

I understood when I went to the toilet after lunch. Poppy and Lexi were in there, talking about the tests. Poppy kept saying she was hyperventilating (she wasn't) and Lexi was rubbing her back. I had a wee, washed my hands, and left them to it.

With all their drama, they reminded me of Meg. And she was the biggest drama queen in the world.

Thursday 13th July
One more day of silence before we're back to normal. I say normal but tomorrow's Sports Day. There's nothing normal about that. For the sporty people, they get to live their best lives and wear a PE kit all day. They get to run races and jump distances and throw things as far as they can.

For the rest of us, we get to watch! Mostly. Everyone has to take part in something. I've gone with the 100 metres sprint - it's over quickly - and the discus. Standing still and chucking a lump of rubber through the air defo beats working up a sweat.

I'd love to be sportier. In Y6, Ms. Archer said it was unfair how women's team sports weren't represented equally on TV. I found myself agreeing with her. But not enough that I want to run around a field chasing a ball with a stick. (That's hockey, if you hadn't worked it out.)

So bring on Sports Day. Its slogan should be, 'Better than tests but only just.'

Friday 14th July

Today was brilliant. Surprisingly so. Who knew I'd enjoy Sports Day! (I didn't do much sport, tbh.) I'm too tired to write another word except to say that Jake wore his Jack Grealish hairband to school for the first time. I overheard Poppy saying how good he looked. **SHUT UP POPPY**.

Saturday 15th July

So, Sports Day. I came 6th out of 8 in the 100 metres (better than I thought I'd be) and I threw the discus 11 metres. But none of that matters because I've been invited to a party.

That isn't why Sports Day was good, btw. The party was an extra thing that happened. The main thing was sitting with Jake, Bella, and James, and talking all afternoon. We chatted like people do in films. Films that are about high school students. We covered all sorts - the teachers we like and those we can't stand, (Mr. Davies came out badly) funny things that have happened this year, (when Lexi screamed at a bee and ran out of the room) and what we're doing over the summer, (me - nothing, James - going to Italy!) Every so often one of us would nip off to do a sport and then come back and lie on the grass. The rest of the time, we made daisy chains. Jake's went from his foot to his hip. It took him ages.

But the party! Yes, James is having a party. It's the day we break up. Everyone's invited including me. I cannot believe it. I'm finally getting a life.

Sunday 16th July
It occurred to me that Mum might be funny about me going to James.' Especially as his parents won't be there. Actually that's not true. They'll be there at the start but then they're going for their anniversary meal. They've said he can have his friends over, although I don't think they meant the whole of Class 1. Hopefully they won't come back to find the place trashed. That's what would happen in a film.

I've just realised that everything I know about high school parties comes from films. Like the ones from the 1980s that Mum likes. I can't imagine what a Lake District party in the now times will be like.

Monday 17th July
Period.

Everyone's got a 'last week of term' feeling. No one can be bothered, including the teachers, and the days are filled with jobs. At home, if you asked me to tidy, I'd complain for ages. At school, it's way better than the alternative.

In the lesson that should've been Maths, Miss Wilkinson gave me a staple extractor and told me to pull all the staples out of the wall. It was well good.

Tuesday 18th July
What do people wear to parties? I don't think I have anything right. The party clothes in Mum's high school films are from years ago. None of my clothes look like that.

Wednesday 19th July

I asked Jake. I thought he might be helpful. 'What are you wearing to James' party?' I said. I couldn't have been clearer. He barely looked up before saying, 'Clothes I think.' I rolled my eyes. 'No really, what are you wearing?' He looked up that time. He'd been trying to open his yoghurt without it exploding onto his shirt, but it'd happened anyway. He sighed. 'Whatever's clean.' That's when I groaned. 'Are you being deliberately annoying?' I said. He looked surprised. 'No! What do you want me to say? It'll be my jeans and a hoody. Except if it's warm, it'll be a t-shirt. Maybe my light blue polo.'

I guess he was helpful in the end. He showed me he's not stressing over what he wears. I wish I wasn't. Because whatever I choose, Poppy and Lexi will have comments.

Thursday 20th July

Mum has a phrase. I can't remember it. It's when women are nasty about other women because society has taught them it's OK to treat women badly. And even though it's the same as being nasty to themselves, they don't see it that way. Mum says Grandma's always doing it. Usually when she describes someone as being 'the wrong shape for that outfit' or when she says, 'Did she put her make up on in the dark?' That sort of thing. I'll ask Mum when she comes up to bed. Meanwhile I've got my leggings and my denim shirt dress on a hanger. I like those clothes and that should be all that matters. Obvs it's not, but I'll keep telling myself that it is.

Mum's just come up. Women hating on other women is called internalised misogyny. How am I supposed to remember that?

Friday 21st July
Break up for summer.

Before I fell asleep last night, Mum asked me why I wanted to know about internalised misogyny. I said I needed to spell it right for my diary. She said, 'Looks like I've trained you well.'

That made me want to write something sarky about how it's nothing to do with her and everything to do with Poppy and Lexi. But then I'd be doing my own internalised misogyny on another woman (Mum). That's just as bad as Poppy and Lexi making nasty comments about my clothes. Sometimes the world is complicated.

The good news is, no more Y7! Woohoo. I'm back from school and chilling before the party. Tbh, I feel nervous. I'm not used to parties, or going out with school people. It's been just me and Jake since I moved here. But it's time to - here's an adult saying - spread my wings! Yep, it's time to do something adventurous. And it's not like going to James' house is an actual adventure. I'll still be in Applemere. But that doesn't stop me feeling nervous and excited, all at once.

The other cool thing is I'm sleeping at Jake's. Mum said that we could walk back to his together but I can't walk home from there on my own. Not late at night. I moaned for a bit because I thought she was trying to stop me going, but no. She'd already sorted it with Cait. I'll be in Jake's room while he gets the sofa.

My wings are ready to fly and I'm about to have the biggest adventure of my life. Time to get ready for my party and sleepover.

Saturday 22nd July

Hmmm. Not sure what to write. Might leave it till tomorrow.

Sunday 23rd July

At some point I'll work out what I'm feeling. Just not sure when that'll be. Sorry Auction Bidders. I'll get back to you.

Monday 24th July

Spike was upset this morning because of his carrots. He dug them up thinking they'd be huge but they turned out to be tiddlers. Dad said that was the style of carrot they'd planted but Spike thought it was because he was a bad planter. I walked in to the living room to find Mum stroking his head. She said, 'Everything will feel better tomorrow. It always does.'

It's a nice idea but it's not true. It's been three days since everything went weird and it still doesn't feel better. Maybe it never will?

Tuesday 25th July

'Little Women' is finally finished. It took a while but I understand it better after the party. Being a girl with a boy best friend has always been complicated. Even in the olden days with Jo and Laurie. Am I Jo? Is Jake, Laurie? No. Because that means he'd have to marry Harvest and that's hilarious.

Wednesday 26th July

Everything's still weird. Poppy is HORRIBLE. She's wrecked everything good about me and Jake. Spin the bottle is such a stupid game. IT'S ALL HER FAULT.

Thursday 27th July

I guess I'll try and explain. It might help to write it down. Get my thoughts on paper. You never know.

Friday night was going fine. I was wearing my denim dress and I'd even done eyeliner after watching a YouTube video. It looked good (well it did after I'd wiped off the first few tries). Me and Jake walked down the lane to James' and everything felt OK. Poppy was there, obvs, but I had a plan. Smile, then give her space for the rest of the night. It worked too. For the first couple of hours.

It was after James' parents had gone out and everyone was in the living room. Poppy stood on the sofa, (in her trainers!) told Alexa to stop playing, and said, 'Right everyone, time for spin the bottle! Make a circle on the floor and get ready for some tonsil tennis!'

I knew what spin the bottle was but I'd never played it. Kissing is what other people do. People who have boyfriends and girlfriends, and who talk in the toilets after they'd been dumped. I'm sure Poppy's kissed lots of people. And when Lexi and James were together, they sometimes kissed on the field at lunch time. I've never done that but I sat in the circle anyway. So did Jake.

It didn't happen straight away. Poppy went first and spun the Coke bottle. It landed on Owen. He looked terrified for a second before shrugging. She laughed her head off and they moved towards each other. I didn't think they'd actually do it, but they did. It was only a peck but everyone cheered. Well, Lexi did. A few others joined in. Then they moved back to the circle and it was Owen's turn to spin. I was still thinking how silly it was, when the bottle landed on me.

I'm not stupid. If I didn't want to play, I shouldn't have sat in the circle. I walked on my knees towards Owen, kissed him on the mouth for half a second, and went back to my place. It didn't feel bad but it didn't feel exciting either. It was just a peck and it was over in no time. Then it was my turn.

'Spin the bottle, Leeza. Let's see who's next!' shouted Lexi. I spun it, hoping it wouldn't land on Poppy. Kissing girls is fine if it's what you want to do, but defo not Poppy. That was all I could think about as I watched the bottle slow down. When it stopped, I looked up to see who I'd got. Obvs. You've guessed it... Jake.

I laughed straight away. As IF I was going to kiss Jake. But then Poppy started clapping and shouting, 'Leeza and Jake, Leeza and Jake,' as she stared daggers at me. Everyone else joined in. Jake just looked embarrassed.

I tried to think how to get out of it but suddenly we were crawling towards each other. It happened without my brain realising. By then we'd got to the middle of the circle. Jake paused to push his hair away from his eyes and next thing you know, we were kissing. Actually kissing! For MORE than a second.

The rest of the evening felt blurry. We laughed it off at the time and the game carried on but I'd stopped having fun. I didn't really speak to Jake and kept out of his way. When it was time to walk back to his flat, there was an awkward silence. Neither of us knew what to do. I didn't sleep much and got away as fast as I could the next morning.

Before Friday, if you'd have asked me who Jake was, I'd have known straight away. My best mate. The one person I can be myself with. Now? If you asked me the same question, I have no idea. Everything feels wrong. I HATE IT.

Friday 28<u>th</u> July
I came downstairs to see Harvest and Spike watching Mr. Tumble. Since his carrots disaster, he's been

quieter than usual. For some people this would be a worry but with Spike it's well nicer. Obvs when he saw me watching he told me to get lost and stop being a loser. It'd be weird if he didn't.

Friday Fooday was veggie spag bol with garlic bread. It was probably lovely but I didn't feel hungry. Besides, it's far too hot for spag bol.

Saturday 29th July

Jake messaged. Not about the party. He said MUM SAYS ASK MOLLY IF SHE WANTS TO GO FOR A DRINK NEXT SAT. HER PHONE'S DED SO SHE TOLD ME TO MSG.

I asked Mum, who was more excited than I've ever seen her. 'I'll be there with bells on,' she said. 'I've not been out for ages and I'm gasping for adult conversation.' Dad muttered, 'Charming,' under his breath as she carried on. 'Tell Cait to brace herself because it's going to be epic. She won't know what's hit her when I get away from you lot.' I didn't tell her any of those things because I was telling Jake. Instead, I was polite and to the point. MUM SAYS YES. IT'S ON THE CALENDAR.

Looking back, I could have been friendlier. It's hard. We haven't had a row. We've just got ourselves into an awkward place. I don't know how to get back to where we were.

Sunday 30th July
Jake replied with a thumbs up emoji. He was only passing on messages for his mum but it still felt harsh. I thought about messaging today in a friendlier way but I gave up after a few tries. I sounded fake. This is the way things are now.

There was one bit of distraction tonight. After a week of sweltering weather, it finally rained. Or as Dad said, 'It persisted it down.' The rain started this afternoon but by evening it was full on thunder.

This was immediately brilliant. I LOVE thunder. When the lightning comes, I like to watch from the window and wait for the sky to light up. It's well better than the telly. That's what was going through my mind after we heard the first roll. But then I remembered. Blane is terrified of thunder.

He started to cry, then crawled behind the sofa. His cries got louder and he was getting all het up. Mum and Dad were upstairs putting clothes away but they heard him. Mum shouted, 'Don't worry Blane. It can't hurt you inside,' then carried on with what they were doing. Her words made no difference, of course.

How do you deal with a child who's frightened of thunderstorms, slap bang in the middle of a massive thunderstorm? There was only one thing to do. Watch 'Paddington 2' of course.

It wasn't new. We've seen it before. But this time something brilliant happened. Within a few minutes, Blane stopped crying. Then he emerged from the sofa so he could see the TV. Spike was at his most grown up and helped Harvest onto the cushions so she could watch too. Kenny - who'd been building a block tower at the table - stopped what he was doing and came and joined us. By the time Paddington was in the barber's getting carried away with the clippers, we were all cuddled under the tartan blanket, completely forgetting about the weather. After a while, Blane even began to laugh.

When Mum and Dad came down, I got a 'thanks Leeza' before they went and put the kettle on. If I'm being honest, I'd say that wasn't enough, but I was too busy enjoying the film to notice. Laughing at Paddington with my brothers and sister, was exactly what I needed. Thanks Blane. Your terror of weather helped me loads.

Monday 31st July

I'd enjoyed last night's film so much that I watched it again this morning. You can tell it's the summer holidays and I'm starting to get bored.

8

Problem Solving On High

<u>Tuesday 1st August</u>

Dad woke me with a question. 'What happened a year ago this week?' I shouldn't have to use my brain before my eyes are open. 'Come on Leez, what did we do a year ago? You too, Spike.' He shouted into his room. 'What happened the first week of August last year?' By the time Dad had woken everybody, I'd got it. Last August we moved to Applemere Bridge. Time has absolutely flown.

Actually, I've got that wrong. It feels like I've been here forever. If time had flown, it'd only feel five minutes since we arrived. Considering how worried I was about moving, it's turned out all right.

Wednesday 2nd August

I said that to Mum. 'It feels like we've been here ages.' She looked up from her laptop. 'That's because Cait and Tom were so welcoming. And look how Jake helped you.' Then she went back to her screen.

I shouldn't have opened my mouth. Later, when I was waiting for Kenny to finish in the bathroom (that kid poos for ages!) Mum shouted downstairs to Dad, 'Let's get Cait and Tom over on Friday! To thank them for their help.' 'Good idea,' Dad shouted back.

If Tom and Cait are here, we know who else will be coming. Great. (Sarcasm!)

Thursday 3rd August

I was thinking about the psychology that Dad taught me. When someone feels scared, they fight, fly away, faint, or freeze on the spot. I thought about how I act when I see Jake.

I haven't fainted. Not so far anyway. I don't think I freeze because when he messaged about Cait and Mum's night out, I messaged back. I've not fought him

\- I've been extra polite if anything. So maybe the closest thing is I've flown away. Maybe flying away from problems is something I do now.

Not for real, obvs. Although that would be nice. No, I've just kept my distance. I've not seen him since the party and other than a few messages, we've not chatted. That'll stop tomorrow when he's here for tea.

If I had any other friends, I could pretend I had plans. Annoyingly, Jake was all I had.

Friday 4th August

I've decided. I'm going to be as normal as possible. I'm going to smile. I'll chat to Cait and Tom and I'll stay at the table instead of going off with Jake. The last thing I want is for us to be alone and not know what to say. I'm wearing my favourite leggings and I'm about to try eyeliner again. (I still need YouTube for help.) By the time they arrive, I'll be looking great and feeling… OK.

Hopefully.

Saturday 5th August

Well Auction Bidders, I got through it. Just.

Mum and Dad have finally realised it's summer, so there was salad, hummus, garlic potatoes, and crusty bread. Even though it was the best meal I've had this week, I couldn't eat much. I was too busy fake-smiling and asking Mum and Cait about their plans for tomorrow. Anything to keep the conversation feeling safe.

Cait had brought non-alcoholic beer. Mum stopped at one glass of wine. According to Dad, that doesn't bode well for their night out. 'Don't be ringing for a lift because you can't walk straight. I'm not waking the kids for a thirty second trip down the road.' We all hope she doesn't do that.

Tom said, 'There's always the sofa if you want to stay. Not bad, is it lad?' Jake shrugged. Cait said, 'Your Leeza was the perfect house guest. Not a peep out of her the whole time. Snuck out before breakfast too.' Mum said, 'You're joking? She's a nightmare to wake up. Especially in the holidays.' Cait said, 'She was gone before I was out of the shower. Good job, really. I'd forgotten the cereal.'

As they carried on, Jake and me had eye contact. Only a second. It's hard to know what he was thinking but he looked... sad. That's how I feel too.

(It's 11.46pm and Mum's still out.)

Sunday 6th August
Mum was hungover. I came down to find Dad banging the cupboard doors on purpose and telling Kenny to sing her a song. Next thing, 'Wheels on the Bus' is coming from the living room and Dad's laughing his head off. I don't want to do an internalised misogyny (I've checked back for the spelling!) but she looked rough. 'Leave me to my Berocca, you horrors,' she groaned. Then she slumped down on the sofa and closed her eyes.

She was better by this afternoon. She came into my room while I was reading and started looking through my wardrobe. 'Does your cossie still fit? It's been a couple of years since you've worn it.' 'Not sure,' I said.

I don't think I'm taller but my boobs are defo bigger than two years ago. I didn't say that, obvs. Too embarrassing. 'I'll look for a new one,' she said to herself. Then without her voice changing she said, 'Everything OK between you and Jake?'

I dropped my book and lost my place before scrabbling about trying to find the page. 'Fine,' I said. She carried on looking at my clothes and pulling out hangers. 'Me and Cait were talking last night...' my face burned, '...and we thought you both seemed quiet. Has something happened?'

I was getting annoyed now. It's none of her business what's happened with Jake. People are allowed to spend less time together and not have to explain themselves. Eventually I said, 'Nothing's happened. It's fine.'

Then she really went for it. 'Is this one of the times I have to read your emails because I'm worried about you?' I looked her straight in the eye, pushed down the fury inside, and said, 'If you do, all you'll see is me and

Jenna talking rubbish.' She looked at me for a moment, before saying, 'OK,' and going downstairs.

Phewwww. The good thing is, that's true. There's nothing in my inbox except emails from Jenna. And not that many of those since I got my phone. The real worry is if she reads my diary. She might as well just crawl into my brain and find all my deepest feelings. I will not let that happen.

Monday 7th August

I've never worried about my diary before. No one sees me write it because I do it before bed. I'm not stupid. I move its hiding place around. In Stockford, it was kept between folded clothes I'd grown out of. No one looked there. In Applemere I've used a couple of places. Under my mattress and on top of my wardrobe (I stand on my chair.) If Mum or Dad were to stretch up high, they could reach it, but I don't see why they would.

Not unless they're worried about me. I'll just have to stop them worrying in the first place.

Tuesday 8th August

I've got a plan.

If Mum's worried and wants to read my emails, I should let her. There's nothing to see. I checked my inbox today. The ones I've kept are funny threads with Jenna. I moan - quite a lot – about family stuff but nothing that would get me in trouble. And if you can't moan to your mates about things that get you down, there's something wrong.

My plan is to leave myself logged in, just before Mum uses the iPad. She'll see my inbox and not be able to stop herself. Hopefully it'll calm her down and she'll get over this 'Jake' thing.

I'm officially angry. In order to keep my privacy, I have to pretend I've forgotten to keep things private. **HOW STUPID**. Maybe I should read Mum and Cait's emails too. I bet there's all sorts in there.

Wednesday 9th August

So far, my plan hasn't worked. I've left the iPad by Mum TWICE. Both times, Spike has swiped it from under her nose and both times I've had to run after him to log out.

I suppose the good thing is I've not thought about Jake for a couple days.

<u>Thursday 10th August</u>
There's more stress coming my way. My stomach has started its old trick. It's full of butterflies, or as I like to call them, stompy elephants. (It's the wrong time for period flutterings.) Something's going on and I don't know what it is.

Mum's been on her phone all day. I know it's not work. Dad's been busy upstairs, but she's been down here constantly messaging someone. Grandma rang at one point and Mum answered straight away. That never happens. And what's more, she said, 'Hey Ma,' and then walked outside and had a conversation on the drive. They never talk in private. We hear everything they say. Either because Mum tells Dad how Grandma's annoyed her or because they're shouting and the whole house can hear.

Secret chats are new. And worrying. If that wasn't enough, Mum's just knocked on my door. 'Family meeting on Sunday. Kitchen table, 3pm.'

I feel sick.

Friday 11th August

This is supposed to be the summer holidays. No school, no worries, just lots of fun. How am I supposed to relax? I've kissed my best mate and it's gone weird, Mum's keeping secrets from us, and there's still too many people in my face.

When my head gets like this, I usually go to Jake's. Instead I'm stuck inside with my feelings.

That's why I did it. It was only a few seconds. No one saw me. But I still feel bad.

Saturday 12th August

I only went and looked at Mum's phone, didn't I. I know, Auction Bidders. It wasn't right. I was just wound up with everything. Mum and Grandma keeping secrets, and Mum threatening to read my diary. OK, she didn't say she'd do that but I've worried about it ever since. I didn't feel like I had a choice. And yes, Auction Bidders, I know I had a choice. I shouldn't have done it. But it didn't help. It just made things more confusing.

I only saw one message. I was scared I'd be caught and didn't want anyone clocking the phone in my hand. All I read was the last thing Mum sent Grandma. WE'LL TELL THE KIDS ON SUNDAY. ALSO, J'S BEEN IN TOUCH. D'S NOT GOOD.

That's when I panicked and put down the phone. I left the kitchen as quickly as I could, only moments before Mum walked in saying, 'Anyone seen my phone?' My heart was racing and the sick feeling was back. Who are J and D? And what are we being told tomorrow?

I miss Jake. This is exactly the kind of thing I'd share with him. (Oooh! Is 'J' Jake?)

Sunday 13th August

After another sleepless night (I only got 8 hours instead of my usual holiday 12) I woke up feeling sick and cranky. I was desperate to get 3 o'clock out of the way.

When the time came, I was ready. I was on the edge of my kitchen chair, my hands were clutching the table, and my mouth was dry.

'We've got some news,' Mum began. Not another house move. Not another baby. Not another way to turn my entire world upside down. My mind was running away with itself but Mum carried on. 'We weren't sure if we'd be able to manage it this year but a friend of Gina's has come to our rescue, and...' I had no idea where this was going. What had Mum's college friend got to do with any of this? '...we're going on holiday! Next week, to the Welsh coast, in Gina's friend's caravan. All of us. And Grandma and Will!'

Mum had a big smile. Dad said, 'What do you think about that, kiddos?' Spike shouted, 'YESSSSS.' Blane started to cry, saying, 'These are my happy tears.' Kenny clapped his hands over and over, and Harvest dribbled. I think I was in shock. An actual holiday? It's been ages since we went anywhere. Literally ages.

I smiled at some point. It was relief as much as anything. A holiday by the sea is exactly what I need.

I only had two questions. The first one I asked at the meeting. 'Will Grandma be staying in the caravan?'

Dad laughed as Mum shook her head. 'No, Leez. I don't think any of us want that, especially Grandma. She'll be in a hotel with Will. We'll see them every day but we get our own space at night.' Dad laughed again and said, 'I think that's best for us all.'

The second question I kept to myself. If I'd asked it, it'd be obvious I'd been reading Mum's phone. I get what the first half of the text message meant. 'We're telling the kids on Sunday' was to do with the holiday. But that doesn't answer my other question.

Who are J and D?

Monday 14th August

Dad handed me my toast and said, 'The holiday countdown starts here. We've got five days to wash, pack, and do as much work as we can before we take the week off.'

I'm glad I don't have a job. When I'm older, I'll need one that gives me the whole summer off. (Not a teacher. I don't want to be inside a school any longer than I have to be.) There's bound to be loads of jobs like that. I just have to work out what they are.

Tuesday 15th August
I'm keeping out of Mum and Dad's way. By the time I came to bed, there were four baskets of dried washing, waiting to be folded. Their laundry routine never stops. The machine's going most of the time, often into the night. If I tried to help and fold my own clothes, I'd be in their way. Mum said as much this afternoon. After telling me to get away from the baskets because she didn't want them mixed up, she said, 'If you really want to be helpful, go to Tom's and sort tea.'

I must have looked blank. She said, 'Earth to Leeza, hello. Tea?' I snapped back into action. 'What should I get?' Mum carried on folding Harvest's vests and said,

'I couldn't care less. Whatever you fancy that'll feed us all.'

Sometimes I like being treated like a grown up. But choosing a meal for seven people, from the mini supermarket in a small village, is not fun. And that's before I'd even thought about seeing Jake.

He was on the till when I walked in. Just like the first time we met. Back then I thought he was annoying. Now I wish it were that simple.

The best thing to do, I decided, was be completely normal. 'What do you recommend for an evening meal for a family of 7?' I opened with that. 'I've got my mum's card and I can choose anything.' He laughed. 'Molly's trusted you with that? Quick, let's get spending!'

It was nice to laugh. We knew we were avoiding the party but it was almost the same. Jake suggested seven Pot Noodles and I told him to get lost. (Imagining Harvest trying to eat a Pot Noodle made me lol). Then we settled on pasta. We calculated that for 7 people, we'd need two big bags of shells, two tins of tomatoes, peppers, mushrooms, and some grated cheese. He put everything in a bag, as well as a box of chocolate fingers I decided I deserved. Then I tapped Mum's card.

Things felt lighter on the walk home. Not the bag I was carrying - that dug into my hand the whole way - but the feelings inside.

<u>Wednesday 16th August</u>
I'm sick of being told to stay out of Mum and Dad's way. If they didn't want to be mithered by kids, they shouldn't have had 5, and they shouldn't work from home. I'm just saying.

Mum told me I was being a pain because I said I only needed 7 pairs of leggings and 7 tops. I thought that'd make things easier, but no. 'And will you go swimming in your leggings? Will you go to nice restaurants in your leggings? Will you sleep in your leggings?'

She's lost the plot.

Thursday 17th August

I woke up feeling nervous so I tried to work out what the problem was. The Jake thing is calmer. We've had some space, and when I saw him in the shop, we were OK. It's not sorted but it's easier. It can't be that.

The holiday is exciting and I'm looking forward to it. The day after tomorrow I'll be in a caravan by the sea. It's just what I need to chill out, and thinking about it makes me happy. So it can't be that.

There's ages till we go back to school. I don't have any homework, and I'm not worried. I'll still be in Class 1 so that's fine. It's not that.

The feeling hasn't gone away all day. Annoying.

Friday 18th August

Period.

Well now we know what the feeling in my tummy was. You'd think I'd be used to it. It's been eight months.

I sighed when I clocked I'd come on. But then I had a thought. Going on holiday with a period is a whole new experience. I'll have to make sure I pack enough pads and have spare knickers, just in case. And what about swimming? OMG. This is NOT what I need.

I couldn't see any other way. I had to tell Mum. She rolled her eyes. She's had loads more than 8 periods. Some of them must have come at the wrong time too. 'Don't worry, I'll pack what you need. You'll probably have time at the end of the week for swimming.' 'Yeah,' I agreed. 'I should be done by Wednesday.' Then she said, 'If you want to try tampons, that's OK. You could swim straight away then.'

I like that she'd given me the option, but I shook my head. Maybe another time when I can have a go when I'm relaxed. I don't think a caravan loo with Spike shouting through the walls is the best place.

I'm going to sleep now. At least I'll try. Tomorrow will be brilliant!

Saturday 19th August

I thought about it and I'm going to take my diary. I want to write down everything that happens. I'll just need to find a hiding place in the caravan.

Dad's loading the car. We've each got a binbag for our clothes. They squash in the boot better than cases. Spike's made the same joke loads. He picks up his binbag and says, 'I'll just get rid of this rubbish,' and starts to walk to the wheelie bin. Harvest laughs every time. No one else does.

I'm getting called now. Mum's rinsing her mug and leaving it on the drainer. Spike's doing his binbag joke one more time, and Dad's waiting to get in the car. Harvest is clapping in her car seat. Kenny's climbing into his. Mum's shouting at me to get a move on.

Time to escape to the seaside! Next time you hear from me, I'll be in Wales! Woohoooooo!

Sunday 20th August

I'm having the best time!

Monday 21st August

It's so good to be away! Bear with me, Auction Bidders, I'm too busy eating ice creams, paddling in the sea, and playing in the arcades to write much.

Tuesday 22nd August

I've collected loads of shells and I had fun burying Spike. 'Everywhere but me 'ead!' he kept shouting as we piled on the sand. Tomorrow we're going swimming (finally I can go!) and then a big walk up the cliffs. And we had a chippy tea!

I sleep really well here. Sea air is the best.

Wednesday 23rd August

OK, Auction Bidders, let me tell you about the caravan. I'm sharing a room with Harvest. She sleeps through the night now so it could be worse. Spike, Blane, and Kenny are in another room. Spike's on the drop down bunk bed. There's a kitchen and dining area and a big sofa curving round under the window. It's been sunny every day, so the caravan doors are open and we've eaten our meals on the grass. Sometimes the seagulls try and take food and we have to wiggle our legs to keep them away.

Grandma and Will have been fun. 'Fancy bumping into you lot!' was how she greeted us when we arrived. Will high-fived everyone before saying, 'Right gang, the ice creams are on me,' and leading us to the beach kiosk. Mum and Dad are chilled out too. They took us swimming this morning and spent the whole time splashing and dunking us under the water. They laugh more than at home. I guess having a job means there's less time for fun.

I really enjoyed this afternoon. It was actually perfect. Dad wanted to walk along the coastal path and said we could go too. I didn't mind a short walk but what I really wanted was to look at the sea. I love the water. It sounds weird when I try to explain but it makes me feel calm. Dad didn't mind. He said we'd find a nice place to stop along the way. We set off after lunch.

My leg muscles are not used to climbing. They started to ache really quickly. Part of the path was flat but then out of nowhere it'd suddenly get steep. Like a proper cliff. Just when it felt like my legs couldn't climb any more, the path would go flat again. It kept changing all the time. All the while, I could look down to the right and see the shimmering sea. It was beautiful.

Eventually we got to a flat bit that opened into a grassy space. There were a few benches and picnic tables for walkers that had brought a packed lunch. Obvs we hadn't. I sat on one of the benches, while Dad, Spike, and Blane stretched out on the grass.

I looked at the water. It was a long way down and it stretched out forever. The sun made everything sparkle. I felt completely relaxed in my bones. I never feel that.

It was the best chance I had to sort my head out. And when I say 'my head' I mean, the Jake situation. I sat, and looked, and thought, and breathed, and thought again. Up there, I could think back to James' party without feeling embarrassed. It was safe because I was away from real life. I thought about what I wanted, why it felt weird, and what I needed to do. It was the best think I've had in ages.

I've no idea how long we were there. Maybe ten minutes, maybe an hour. But in that time, everything fell into place. I know what must come next. But that can wait until I'm back home. Thank you, Clifftop! Thank you, Sea! I'll NEVER forget you.

Thursday 24th August

Grandma's dirty secret is out. She's addicted to one of the arcade machines. The one where you put 2p coins in the slot to try and push out more 2ps from the bottom. Mum had to tell her to walk away. 'But I have to win my money back!' she said, as Will guided her out.

It's Spike's birthday tomorrow and even I'm excited about it. Everything's fun here, even my brother's birthday.

Friday 25th August

Spike is 9!

The first thing I heard was Spike bouncing up and down the caravan shouting, 'Wake up, wake up, the best day of the year has arrived. You are my servants and I am the boss.' Yeah, right, I thought. I rolled over but a few minutes later I needed a wee. I had to get up.

Mum was sitting in the kitchen area with a coffee. She was ignoring Spike too, even though he was still banging on. He was wearing a chef's hat and a red apron that said SPIKE in white letters. 'Best let him get it out of his system, yeah?' I nodded and got myself some cereal. 'Why's he wearing that?' I asked. Mum yawned before saying, 'It'll be good for him to learn to cook the veg he's grown. Keep him out of trouble.' That's a mistake. Spike should not be near knives.

I changed the subject. 'What are we doing today?' I asked. Mum looked straight at me. 'Don't ask me. Ask the boss.' She nodded towards Spike. Obvs I wasn't doing that so I took my cereal outside and watched the seagulls. It was a lovely start to the day. (Apart from Spike.)

I'll write more tomorrow. Who knows what I'll be made to do later.

Saturday 26th August

Who knew Spike would have a good idea? Tbh it was Grandma. I don't think she fancied leaving Spike in charge of her eating plans. When he told her he was the boss of the day, she looked horrified. I know how she felt but I thought a grandmother would make more effort to hide her annoyance. I laughed about the look on her face whenever I remembered.

While we were walking back from the beach, I heard Grandma chatting behind me. 'Spike, my darling, what have you decided for our evening meal?' 'Evening meal' is another way Grandma says 'tea'. Like she's the Queen or something. He said, 'I told Mum. Beans and chips. We'll eat in the caravan. You and Will too.' There was silence behind me. We kept walking. Then I heard Grandma say, 'How marvellous. Although, I wonder if there's enough room for everyone around that poky seating area. Why don't we make a big effort for your special day. What about coming for a meal at my hotel? I'll pay. It faces the beach so we can watch the sunset and they have lovely seats with lots of space. More importantly they have gin and tonic. I'll be wanting a large one of those.'

I laughed to myself. There's no way Grandma was ever going to eat in the caravan. She hasn't done that all week.

We all dressed up. I wore my strappy sun top with my denim skirt and Mum wore a maxi dress I've never seen before. Dad even sprayed aftershave. It was fine when it was just him but then Spike, Blane, and Kenny got a spray too. We had to leave the caravan before we choked on the fumes. The walk along the beach was lovely and before we knew it, we'd arrived at the hotel.

Grandma greeted us like SHE was the boss of the day. 'You made it! Come in! We've got a lovely table in the bay window.' Tbf to her, it was well nicer than oven chips in the caravan. A waiter came to take our orders and told Spike that baked beans were definitely on the kids' menu. Spike's grin was massive.

But the best part was when Mum let me choose from the adult menu. When you've dealt with a period in a caravan, you're ready for an adult meal. I had a halloumi burger with chilli mayo, and skin on fries. It was AMAZING. I also had my lemonade in a wine glass. It was the BEST night.

We got back to Applemere a couple of hours ago. The washing machine's going. I can hear Dad in the kitchen supervising Spike. Kenny's just gone to bed and is having a little cry. I know how he feels. I always feel like crying when something brilliant is over. Maybe I'll do that in a bit.

Sunday 27<u>th</u> August
Yeah. I did have a cry. For a few minutes, once I knew everyone was busy. It felt good.

Monday 28<u>th</u> August
Now the holiday's over, I've got to face reality. It's nearly back to school time. If I had the space, I'd write BOOOOOOO so it filled the entire page. That's how strongly I feel.

The good news is, no more Poppy. She'll be next door in Class 2. Woohoo! The bad news? No more Jake. I'll see him on the bus, but he won't be with me at school. Maybe that's for the best.

I still have to sort out the Jake situation but that's for another day. Meanwhile, Harvest has learnt a new trick. With the help of Spike and Mr. Tumble, she can make animal sounds. I found this out when I was trying to read. All I could hear was Spike saying, 'Go on Harv, do the lion, do the lion.' A second later, her little voice would go, 'Raahhh.' They did that all afternoon. Neither of them got bored.

Tuesday 29th August

Jake messaged. MUM'S SORTING OUT THE LOFT. DOES SPIKE WANT MY OLD CLOTHES? SIZE 9-11.

I asked Mum, who didn't pause for breath. 'Hell yeah. Spike goes through T shirts like the Hulk.' I didn't tell Jake that, but I was friendlier than last time. MUM'S MADE UP. SHE SAYS SHE'LL DEFO TAKE THEM IF CAIT'S SURE. SPIKE WILL HAVE NEVER LOOKED SO COOL. I added a crying laughing emoji. I was making fun of Spike, not flirting with Jake. The emoji did the job.

As an afterthought, I sent a vid from yesterday. It was Harvest sitting on the couch going, 'Raahhh,' with hand gestures. Jake would like it.

I got a row of crying laughing emojis back, so that was nice.

Wednesday 30th August

Something bad has happened. Well, it's bad for Dad. He got a call from his mum. We were watching 'Escape to the Country' when I heard the phone go upstairs. I carried on watching. After a while, Mum came down and told us.

Grandma Jeanette had rung to say that Dad's dad is sick. Mum said Dad had known he was ill but now it's serious. Spike asked the question I was too scared to say. 'Will he die?' He came out with it, just like that. Mum thought about it for a second before answering. 'I'm afraid it looks that way. In a month or two, maybe more. The doctors have tried everything but he's been sick for a long time.'

I don't know what to feel. I don't even feel comfy calling him Grandad Dougie because he wasn't there when we visited. He's a stranger but I still feel sorry for Dad.

His plan is to drive across tonight and hope to visit tomorrow. He doesn't know if his dad will want that, but it's worth a try. To lighten the mood, Mum said, 'On top of that, Dad's staying at Grandma's. God help him if he makes a mess. She'll be after him with her Dustbuster.' We laughed and she went back upstairs.

Later, we waved off Dad as he backed out of the drive. It felt strange. A week ago I was sitting on a cliff top being the most relaxed I've ever felt. Now, I don't know what to feel. Nothing, I suppose.

Thursday 31st August

We went to the pub for tea. Mum said, 'There's no way I'm doing the dishes on my own. Get your shoes on, kids. We're eating out.'

Tom was at the bar. He must have known what had happened because he was extra kind. He said, 'What'll it be? My round, Molly, you need a stiffener.' Mum smiled. 'Don't I wish, Tom. A large G and T next time but I'll take a lime and soda for now.' He laughed and asked the rest of us what we were having. I got lemonade. No wine glass this time.

It was while we were eating that Mum said it. She'd been talking about Dad. He'd messaged to say he'd been with Grandma Jeanette all day and was going to the hospital tomorrow. He still didn't know how his dad would react. Mum finished her mouthful of pasta and said, 'If nothing else, this is a good lesson for us all. Always sort out arguments before things get out of hand. If you fall out with a family member or...' she looked right at me '... a friend, it's never good to let it drag. Your dad knows that now. Sort it out, soon as.'

Spike said 'What are you raving on about?' but I knew. She was talking to me. And I AM going to sort it. Soon.

9

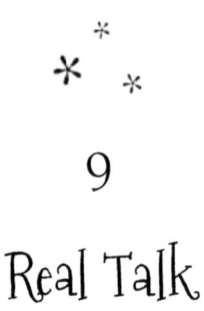

Real Talk

Friday 1st September

Before we left the pub Tom shouted across, 'I'll send the lad down. Give 'im any jobs you need.' Jake turned up at 10am. I saw him through the window, crouched on the grass. Spike was showing off the herbs.

As well as Spike's plants, Jake watched CBeebies with Harvest and listened to her animal sounds. (Raaahhh, miaaooowww, moooooo, and wooooofff.) After lunch, he watched Blane and Kenny ride their bikes.

'I DO like Jake, you know.' Mum snuck up on me as I was filling my I LOVE SCOTLAND mug with water. 'He's kept them quiet all morning. No fights, no tears,

I've not had to deal with anything.' 'Great,' was all I said. He should try doing it all summer and see if it's so easy. 'Have you patched things up yet?' She asked so casually that I answered without thinking. 'No. But I will.'

Arggghhh. She tricked me into sharing private stuff. I do NOT like Mum knowing what's in my head. I'll be extra careful from now on.

Before Jake left, I took control. It was time. 'We need to talk,' I said. It sounded like I was in a soap opera. Jake laughed and so did I. I tried again. 'I didn't mean it to come out like that but we need to. Not now. Another time?'

He answered immediately. 'Course we can. But this weekend's no good. Mum and Grandad are around.' Jake put on a voice and said, 'Let's check our schedules and get back to each other.' He paused for a second. 'You OK? I know I've upset you.'

He looked worried so I shook my head. 'I'm fine. But I know I've upset you.' He smiled and said, 'Look at us.

Sorting it out already. It'll be easy when we finally chat.'

As he walked away from the house, he said, 'Tell Spike I'm never giving him a piggyback again. He's wrecked me.' He stretched, pulled a face, and we laughed.

<u>Saturday 2nd September</u>
Dad got home this afternoon. He looked tired. Blane made a sign that said WELCUM HOM DAD. I wanted to correct the spelling but I didn't. He'd done it himself so I shouldn't meddle.

He found a blob of Blu Tack on the kitchen wall - it's been there since Christmas - and stuck the sign to the front door. Dad walked in a couple of hours later. The first thing he said was, 'Molly, thanks for the poster. I could tell you made it because of the excellent writing!' Blane's smile was massive.

Dad was only fibbing. Mum's writing is nothing like Blane's. I suppose when you're a parent, you have to tell good lies sometimes. Sneaky.

Sunday 3rd September

The last lie in of the holidays. Goodbye bed. You're my favourite thing.

We had an accidental family meeting over lunch. It just happened. Spike started it. Out of nowhere he said, 'Is your dad dead yet?'

Dad choked on his sandwich so Mum had to bang his back. After he'd caught his breath, he said, 'Fair play, mate. Right to the heart of the matter.' He had a swig of Blane's juice and then thought how to answer.

Tbf, the answer's easy. He's still alive. But Dad wanted us to know everything. He started with, 'Grandma Jeanette sends her love to everyone. She said she often thinks of us and I told her we'd visit again soon.' He paused and Mum rubbed his back. For support or because of the choking, who knows? He carried on. 'I saw my dad in the hospital. He'll be there a few more days, then go home. A nurse will visit every day to give him medicine and make sure he's comfortable.'

He looked sad. I had questions but they all sounded wrong. But nothing could be worse than 'Is he dead yet?' so I took the chance.

'Was he pleased to see you or was it weird? Did he look like you remember? Did you make friends?' I didn't want to overload him so I stopped there. Dad cleared his throat and said, 'He was sleepy when I got there so there wasn't a lot of chat. Not from him anyway. Grandma Jeanette told him I'd arrived, then she left and I sat next to him. I told him about you lot. I told him where we live and how work's going. He grunted a few times. He definitely smiled when I told him about his grandchildren.'

That was nice to hear.

Later, I had a thought. Was that one of those times that adults tell kind lies to kids? I think it probably was.

Monday 4<u>th</u> September
Back to school.

This morning was a massive rush. I was late for my bathroom slot - Spike took ages - and now Kenny's at school, there's an extra body to wash. I had to run for the bus. I do not like starting a new term all sweaty and out of breath.

Other than that, it was back to normal. There are new Y7s with us in Class 1 and Jake and the Y9s are next door. I tried not to think about them and concentrated on lessons.

He came over at home time. 'What're you doing on Thursday?' he asked. Based on Miss Wilkinson's lecture today, a pile of homework. She expects more now we're not the babies of the school. Instead I said, 'Nothing. Why?' 'It's Mum's night at college and Grandad'll be in the shop till late. You could come round.' My stomach lurched for a second but my head took charge. I remembered my cliff top thoughts and everything I had to say.

'Cool,' I said. 'Nice one,' he said back.

Next thing, Owen's showing him something on TikTok and they're giggling about whatever it is. In no time, we were back in the village and I was walking down the lane.

I got home to find Mum baking brownies. 'Woohooo,' I said. She looked up. 'Back off, Greedy Guts. These are for Jake. His birthday's coming up and I'm still grateful he kept the little'uns busy while Dad was away.'

It was nice of Jake to help and it's defo his birthday on Wednesday. But seriously? Brownies for one day of helping? If that's the deal, I'm owed all the brownies in the world.

Tuesday 5th September
It was quiet in English. I swear I could hear Poppy's laugh through the wall. I knew she was loud but I didn't think it'd travel though bricks.

Wednesday 6th September
Jake is 14!

14 sounds grown-up. It IS grown-up. I gave him his card at the bus stop. It was a rush job using Blane's glitter pens. Most of them had dried up so it wasn't my best work. Then I handed over the tub of brownies. 'From Mum. To say thanks for helping as well as Happy Birthday.' I made it clear it wasn't me that had gone to that much effort. 'Molly, you legend!' Jake shouted. He ate one straight away. I could still taste my toothpaste so said no when he offered me one.

Tom had decorated the windows of the shop. Full of baby photos of Jake! I spotted them as soon as I arrived for the bus. He couldn't stop blushing. 'I'm going to kill Grandad! He's dead when I see him.' He kept saying it, but deep down he was pleased. It's nice when people make a fuss, even when it's embarrassing.

Ngl, Jake was a cute kid. I can see he's a good looking 14-year-old too. None of this helps my head for tomorrow. The Big Chat. I can't get distracted and forget what I'd decided. That's the last thing I need.

I've practised what I'm going to say. Like lines in a play. It's the best way.

Thursday 7th September

I told Mum I was going for a walk. 'I might pop into Jake's while I'm out. See how Class 2's going.' She was busy drying the big pan. 'Go for it,' she said, without looking up.

He let me in straight away. He must have been waiting by the door. 'D'you want a juice?' he said. I shook my head. I was nervous and knew I'd spill.

We sat on the sofa. My stomach was flipping but I forced it to get a grip. I remembered my lines, took a deep breath, and opened my mouth. 'I just wanted to say...' The words were barely out before he jumped in. He hadn't even heard me start.

'I'm sorry Leeza. That stupid party. I should never have played spin the bottle. I didn't want to make it weird by walking off but then it felt weird anyway. And I feel bad that kissing you felt weird. Because that's insulting and I don't mean it to be. It would've felt weird with anyone, especially with the others clapping and shouting. Sorry, too many weirds. All I keep thinking is that we're just good mates. But then I feel bad in case you *want* to kiss and stuff. I don't want to mess up our friendship but I don't want a girlfriend. I like how we are. How we were. I'm gutted it's screwed up. It's my fault. I shouldn't have played that stupid game.'

He stopped talking and sank back into the sofa. (It's not just me who overuses the word weird!) His eyes were glistening and his cheeks were red. I couldn't wait, not after I'd rehearsed so much. 'Do you want to hear what I've got to say? I've got a whole speech planned.' He looked at me, still red. 'Yeah, course. Soz for going on.'

'I just wanted to say...' I repeated, '... that I thought spin the bottle would be fun. I'd peck a couple of people on the mouth and it wouldn't matter because it was summer and we wouldn't be in school for weeks. But then WE kissed. And we kissed... for REAL.' My mind had a sudden flashback to the kiss. It was soft, and warm, and wet. Quite a nice feeling actually. It was good to get my first kiss out of the way with someone lovely. (The peck with Owen does NOT count!) But that wasn't in my speech. I carried on.

'I've wondered for a while if I've got girlfriend feelings for you. When Poppy gave you the Valentine's card, I was jealous.' He interrupted. 'You should never be jealous of Poppy, no way.' I smiled but carried on. 'And when we kissed, I thought it must be embarrassing because deep down, I had a crush on you. But then I had a proper think...' I paused to remember the cliffs. My happy place. I took a breath, felt calmer, and carried on, '...and the truth is, I just don't feel that way about you. I REALLY like you. You're my best friend and when I'm stressed or sad or when I've got brilliant news, you're the person I want to tell. But I don't want to kiss you or be your girlfriend, or be anything more than besties. I don't think of you like that. And I'm sorry if you do.'

He looked puzzled for a second before I realised. 'Oh, right. You said you don't want that either. Ignore the last bit.' I laughed to myself. Mostly relief, I think.

'You know what this means?' he said. 'We agree! We find each other completely gross and the thought of kissing makes us feel physically sick. Never ever again, McAuliffe!'

I threw a cushion at him, he threw one back, and next thing, we were laughing our heads off. For ages.

After all that stress, we needed to chill. Jake went downstairs to get popcorn. Then we scrolled through Netflix, pointing out what we'd already watched. By the time Tom closed the shop and came up, we were slumped on the sofa. My legs were resting over Jake's, there were cushions everywhere, and two empty popcorn bags on the table.

Friday 8th September

It was a struggle getting up this morning. 'That's the last time you go out on a school night!' Mum shouted from the bedroom. She was busy trying to get a wriggling Kenny into his shorts, without much luck. The boys are taken to school after I've left for the bus. I've no idea if they ever make it on time.

Saturday 9th September

One week back and it's like nothing's changed. I've got a bag full of homework and hundreds of things I'd rather be doing. It doesn't matter. Now me and Jake are sorted, everything feels easier. Not my Maths. That'll never be easy. Just everything else.

Sunday 10th September

'Glad to hear you and Jake have made up,' Mum said as she waggled Spike's toothbrush at him. It was too early for a convo with her. I just nodded and went downstairs.

Later, when I was looking through my planner, she tried again. 'Cait said you had a good evening on Thursday. Tom reckoned you looked like an old married couple on the sofa.'

I refuse to let her wind me up. Everyone thinks we had a lovers' tiff. That's hilarious. At some point I'll tell Jake and we'll laugh that The Mums have got no idea.

Adults think they know everything but sometimes they couldn't be wronger. (Is that a word? Not sure.)

Monday 11th September
Harvest Festival week!

Last year, I knew nothing about harvest time. I'd just moved here, I didn't know anyone, and next thing you know, Mum's having a baby in the village hall.

The Applemere festival isn't until the end of the week. Before that, it's a whole school event. The Y7s are about to learn about crops, community programmes, weather, and farming. It sounds boring when I put it like that, but it's not.

Tuesday 12<u>th</u> September
Jenna is 13!

It's official. I'm a terrible friend. In all the stress of last week, I'd only gone and forgotten Jenna's birthday. **Arggggggh**. I realised first thing when I was writing the date. I felt sick. Then I felt guilty. Then I formed a plan. I told Miss I needed the toilet and snuck my phone out with me. I messaged her as soon as I was in the cubicle. HAPPY BIRTHDAY TO THE BEST PERSON IN STOCKFORD. HOPE YOU'RE HAVING AN EXCELLENT DAY. PRESENT AND CARD ARE IN THE POST.

I know, I know, I lied. I feel terrible. All the Jake drama has messed with my head. After I'd messaged Jenna, I texted Mum. I'VE FORGOTTEN JENNA'S BIRTHDAY. CAN I HAVE A TENNER TO BUY HER A PRESENT?

I saw Mum's reply at lunchtime. SHALL I GET SOME CHOCOLATE FROM THE SHOP? YOU CAN POST IT AFTER SCHOOL.

Panic over. When I got in, there was a box of Maltesers and a Terry's Chocolate Orange on the kitchen table. Jenna messaged as I was writing her card. WOOOHOOO MCAULIFFE, I'M FINALLY A TEENAGER. THNX 4 THE MSG. MISS U.

I need to remember that adults can be helpful. Will I still panic about things when I'm as ancient as Mum? Probably. That'll just be my luck.

Wednesday 13th September

This week it's normal lessons in the morning then harvesting in the afternoon. Food is coming in every day. Not just from students but the community as well.

By the end of the week the donations will be packed in boxes, wrapped in cellophane, and tied with bows. Like gifts. They're given out to old people in the area.

'Old' is a strange word. Mum's old but not enough to get food at Harvest time. Grandma's even older but I can't imagine what she'd do if a school tried to give her a food parcel. They'd never make that mistake twice.

I spent the afternoon wrapping orange ribbon around the finished boxes. Then I had to curl the ends with a pair of scissors. The first few attempts were rubbish but eventually I got the knack. Hopefully my first tries will go to people so old they don't notice.

Thursday 14th September

Doris came to help. She was giving out juice while we worked. 'How's that baby of yours?' she said. 'Good,' I said. 'She can do animal noises now.' 'Bless,' she said. Then carried on with the juice.

One of the new Y7s was standing nearby. She didn't know what to do. 'Do you want to put one of those stickers on each parcel?' I said. I felt sorry for her. That was me last year. If I hadn't had Jake, I don't know what I'd have done. 'Like this?' The girl - Cayla - stuck a sticker on top of the plastic. 'Yep, like that,' I said.

We worked our way along the row of parcels. I curled the ribbons and Cayla stuck the stickers. We didn't chat loads but when Billy dropped a pumpkin and it splattered everywhere, we burst out laughing at the same time.

Friday 15th September
'It's a McAuliffe family night out!' Dad said at breakfast. 'We'll relive every moment of last year, right where it happened.' Spike got up from the table. 'No way, Jose. It was gross.' Blane looked scared, remembering how dramatic it'd been. 'I'll come with you but I'm meeting Jake,' I said, before getting my bag. Mum spoke last, ending the conversation for good. 'Give over, Mac. It was a nightmare from start to finish.'

No one's keen to relive Harvest's arrival.

We walked down the lane after tea. By the time we were in the village there were people everywhere. Cait was on the sweets stall. 'Come and get your E numbers, kids?' she shouted. Doris was selling cakes and called Mum over so she could look at Harvest in the pushchair. Everything smelt lovely and I wished we hadn't eaten.

Mum and Dad joined Tom on the hay bales outside the pub. I found Jake by the drinks stall. Before long we bumped into James and Owen. They'd come with... wait for it... Cayla! Turns out, she lives a few doors down from Owen so had tagged along. It was nice to be able to introduce her to Jake. It showed I was making friends without him.

We mithered Cait until she gave us free strawberry laces and we hassled Tom for some spends. Eventually we ended up on the back field behind the pub.

It's been a long day, Auction Bidders. I'll fill you in on the rest later. Because there's a few things to write down. They're in my head and I want to remember them properly.

Does that make sense? Probably not.

<u>Saturday 16th September</u>
I've just woken up so I'll pick up where I left off.

We'd been chilling on the field for a while. Mostly telling Cayla which teachers were the nicest. James went home first, then Cayla. Once it started to go dark, Owen went too. Jake said, 'There's no point going yet. Grandad'll be here till the pub stops serving.'

In the distance we watched Cait close her stall and join Mum and Dad on the hay bales. They were settling in for the night.

I lay on my back and looked at the stars. There were loads. Impossible to count. Just a dotty shimmer in the far away blue. Jake lay next to me. I could hear his breath in time with mine. It wasn't quite the cliff top but it was just as relaxing.

A moment passed. Jake said, 'Mum was talking about you the other day. Asking why we'd fallen out. She still thinks we were seeing each other.' I groaned. 'My mum keeps fishing too. They need to get lives.' The stars kept twinkling. They were so far away. Jake said, 'Then when I tell her we're not like that, she asks if I'm seeing someone else. She says when she was my age she had loads of boyfriends. She thinks I'm being secretive. Like I've got girlfriends all over the place that I keep to myself.' I rolled my eyes. Obvs Cait would want to know the goss. 'Have you told her that you don't?' He was quiet for a moment. Then he said, 'I've definitely told her I never want a girlfriend.'

Jake's not daft. He knows his own mind. When he says he doesn't want a girlfriend, there's no reason he's wrong. But I carried on. 'I know you feel like that now but you might change your mind. One day you'll meet a girl you like. Maybe not in Applemere but when you go to college or get a job.'

We lay in silence. It lasted too long. The vibe stopped feeling relaxed. Jake's breathing got faster, the air was heavy, and it felt like I'd said the wrong thing. 'Have I said the wrong thing?' I asked. It seemed best to come out with it. 'You don't have to go out with anyone if you don't want. There's no law says you do.'

More silence. I focused on the stars. So pretty. I tried to imagine what it'd be like in space. To look at Earth from way up high. Would I care what was happening in Applemere if it were a speck, millions of miles away. Like being on my clifftop. Far from all my problems. I lay still and thought about that for a moment. That's when Jake spoke. His voice was scratchy but I could hear him.

'I never want a girlfriend because I think I want a boyfriend.'

Sunday 17th September
Harvest is 1!

I've got two memories from Friday night. The first is that as soon as Jake said that, I gave him a hug. It was tricky because we were lying on hard grass and my arms struggled to wrap around him until he rolled over. It didn't matter. I wanted to show I liked that he'd shared his feelings with me. We held each other for ages in a big cuddle.

The second memory is that Mum and Cait chose that exact moment to come and get us. We only knew when we heard Cait's voice shout, 'Remember when we were that age, Molly. Young love. Isn't it sweet? Now get up you two and give us a hand with these benches.'

We scrambled away from each other. The special moment was over. But it's banked in my memories forever.

Harvest's birthday seemed a bit of a let-down after that. Not that she knew what was going on. She wore a sparkly top but had spilt porridge down it within minutes. She clapped as we sang 'Happy Birthday' and when it was time to blow out her candle, she cried until Kenny did it instead.

I think she had fun but my mind was elsewhere.

Monday 18th September
Kenny's full time now. (School's been mornings only so far.) Mum held her hands around Harvest's face and

said, 'Only you to get rid of, my little pumpkin.' I left for the bus without commenting.

My head's still thinking about the other night. I'm so stupid not to realise Jake might like boys. We used to live next to Tim and Ryan. They'd been together for years. And I sounded 100 years old when I said he might meet a nice girl later. That's exactly what Grandma says about Graham Norton.

It was good to see him again. Jake that is, not Graham Norton. 'Does your mum still think we're love's young dream or is that just mine?' I rolled my eyes. It's the best way to deal with Cait's nonsense. He carried on. 'I'm ignoring every comment she makes about us being special friends. She's not big OR clever.' He grinned so I smiled back. 'If my mum wasn't sidetracked with the boys and Harvest, she'd be exactly the same. It's the one good thing about a big family. I'm never the focus for long.'

We ate lunch on the field. Owen and Cayla joined us. Apparently Cayla's dad's just moved out. It'd been brewing for a while but he left in the summer. I said I was sorry but she said she was OK. Jake said, 'You'll still see him. You'll be able to keep in touch when he's not there.' It reminded me of what he said once. That if he had the chance, he'd want to meet his dad.

I moan about my family but I guess I'm lucky. Not lucky. That's too strong a word. But not as unlucky as some people. That's more like it.

Tuesday 19th September
Period.

At lunchtime I went outside. Poppy and Lexi were sitting on the main bench. There are other benches, but you have to walk past the main one first.

As I walked towards them, I heard Poppy say, 'Stop being nasty, Lex. That's a horrible thing to say about Leeza.' Lexi looked surprised. She'd obvs not said anything. It was just Poppy being a cow. I ignored them and walked to the furthest bench I could.

I saw them do the same 'joke' to two others but when Jake walked outside, they were silent. At least I know there's no way he'll go out with her. That's nice to remember when she's being horrible.

<u>Wednesday 20th September</u>
She did it again. Poppy. Outside during lunch.

This time she said, 'That's so mean, Lexi. Leeza can't help how poor she is!' I ignored them and walked to my bench. What a pointless thing to joke about. She should've seen me in Stockford. We were well skinter there.

No one else had come outside and they were desperate for a reaction. As I opened my butties she tried again. In a huge voice, she shouted across, 'Stop it Lexi! That's cruel. It's not her fault her car's like a tin can on wheels.' I looked into the distance and tuned them out. It wasn't about me. Well, maybe in that moment it was, but Poppy was like this with everyone.

Suddenly there was a shout. 'OI! WHAT DO YOU MEAN BY THAT?'

I looked over. Jake was standing behind Poppy. He fumed as he walked to the front of her. 'Apologise to Leeza or I'm telling Miss.' Lexi looked terrified but Poppy tried to style it out. 'I was only having a laugh. She can take a joke, she doesn't mind.'

He looked over at me. I was a bit bewildered. (Great word!) He said it again. 'Go to Leeza and say sorry for being rude. NOW.'

I don't know what he'd have done if she'd refused, but in the end, she did it. She walked over slowly like she was bored and said, 'Soz for making a joke. Blah blah blah. Whevs.' Then she turned round and flounced back to Lexi. A second later they went inside.

Jake sat next to me. 'Is that what you meant, ages ago, when you said she was annoying? I didn't know. I just thought she was... silly. Not actually nasty. Sorry I didn't listen when you said.'

He looked like he'd let me down but he hadn't. Instead he'd sorted out my nemesis once and for all. Well, she didn't give me any hassle for the rest of the day. Win!

Thursday 21st September

Dad's going to Manchester tomorrow. I heard Grandma FaceTiming him when I got in. 'The spare room's ready and our car will be in the garage so you park on the drive. What will you want for breakfast? You must eat, Sebastian, you have to stay strong.'

Dad was doing what I did with Poppy. Tuning her out. While she talked, he was scrolling on his phone under the table. In the end he said, 'Anything's fine, Ursula. Toast, cereal, toad in the hole? I don't care.' She gave him a look and he immediately stopped scrolling. 'I'm just grateful you can put me up,' he said. 'Thank you.'

Ha. Grandma takes no nonsense from anyone.

Friday 22nd September

It was sad to wave Dad off. But the not-sad thing was a chippy tea. Mum really hates being left with dishes.

Saturday 23rd September

Jake came to help. 'Mum says I've to do anything you ask, Molly.' Mum smiled. 'Best news I've heard in ages, love. How are you with bins?' Next thing, he's tying up bin bags in the kitchen and carrying them outside. I would've helped but I'd only just had a shower.

She wasn't done giving orders. 'The main thing is to keep the little ones quiet. Can you entertain them while I'm upstairs?' Because Jake was there, she asked nicely. Usually I'm left to it without even realising.

In the end it was easy. We got everyone on the sofa and watched 'Moana'. Thank goodness for TV. How did olden days people keep kids quiet?

Sunday 24th September
Dad got back late. His dad's at home now. 'Was he OK with you?' Mum asked. She was making tea and I was listening through the door crack. 'More or less.' Dad said. 'He's too weak to kick up a fuss. He liked the photo of the kids though.'

Maybe Dad didn't lie that time.

Monday 25th September
I've got a book from the school library. It's a modern version of 'Little Women' called 'Becoming Jo'. I liked

LW except for how old fashioned it was. Now I've got the perfect book. I started it at lunchtime and was gutted when the bell went.

Tuesday 26<u>th</u> September

I've told Jake he should read 'Becoming Jo'. He'd defo like the humour. Jake pulled a face and said, 'Isn't that a girls' book?' I was SHOCKED. So was he when I let rip at how wrong he was.

'What are you on about, you clown? Books are for everybody! If you start saying some books are for one group of people and other books are for another, you could miss a story that you love. How can you say something's a girl's book? You sound like my grandma!'

He was definitely taken aback. Then he threw his tinfoil at me (it was lunchtime) and held up his hands to give in. 'OK, you win. I'll have a look when you've finished with it. Anything to shut you up.'

It wasn't a row. Just a heated exchange of ideas. But I was right.

Wednesday 27th September

I finished the book last night. I couldn't put it down. Today I handed it to Jake at the bus stop. 'Woah, I thought you'd be ages.' 'Nice try, Woolton,' I said. 'You told me you'd give it a go so now's your chance.'

I'm not sure 'Woolton' is a good nickname for Jake. It's his last name but it sounded silly. When Jenna calls me, McAuliffe, it's got a ring to it. I won't make that mistake again.

Thursday 28th September

I've been watching more makeup tutorials. Every time I try, my eyeliner game gets better. Tonight, I couldn't sleep so I watched someone teach me how to contour. I like wearing make-up now and then but contouring is a whole other level. How do people find the time?

Friday 29th September

Mum sent a text at lunchtime. TELL JAKE HE'S COMING TO FRIDAY FOODAY TONIGHT. CAIT AND TOM TOO. SEE YOU WHEN YOU GET IN.

I told him. He said, 'Mum and Molly are never apart these days. What are we having?' 'No idea,' I said. 'But we can escape to my room later. Remember last time when it was too awkward?' He nodded. 'Yep. When I thought you were into me, and you thought I was into you. But the truth is, I've got a crush on the boy from that TV show we watched, and you're too shouty for anyone to handle?' If there'd been a cushion handy, I'd have launched it at him.

Later in my room, it seemed he'd taken my rant about 'girls' things' to heart. With hardly any encouragement whatsoever - 'make-up's for everyone' - he let me put mascara on him. Then he tried doing flicky eyeliner on me. 'It's well hard,' was what he kept saying as he wiped off his mistakes.

By the end of the night, we'd had a right laugh. Plus I learnt one new piece of information. Jake suits mascara well more than me. Gutted.

<u>Saturday 30th September</u>
So much has happened recently. Dad's dad is hanging on. Mine and Jake's friendship's been like a roller

coaster but we're calmer now. Harvest's moved on from animal noises to saying 'Eeza' when I get in from school, and Poppy's been nowhere near since Jake called her out.

Did I ever find out what I was good at? What do you think? Course I didn't.

10

Grandma x 2

Sunday 1st October

Mum's just said, 'If you don't want to do homework on a Sunday night, don't leave your homework 'til a Sunday night.' She thought she was being funny.

Monday 2nd October

It's all eyes on Harvest now. For ages she's been getting to her feet and holding onto the sofa. A few weeks ago, she started walking along it, keeping both hands on the seats. Now she can stand on her own without holding onto anything.

Dad says we're on Harvest watch. She'll take her first step any day and we don't want to miss it. Spike asked if there was a prize for the person who catches her walking. 'Yes,' said Dad. 'The thrill of seeing your little sister walk for the first time. What could be better?'

Spike's face showed he could think of several things.

Tuesday 3rd October
I ate lunch with Cayla. We sat on the benches and talked about the rest of the class. Not in a horrible way. Just in a 'who sits where, who's friends with who' kind of way. She couldn't believe I'd only lived here a year. 'But you know everything!' she said. It made me laugh.

Wednesday 4th October
Still no walking from Harvest. She stands up, stays on the spot, bends her knees and waves her arms. She can do that for ages.

Other than that, things feel calm. For the first time in ages there's no big drama hanging over me.

Thursday 5th October
Cayla told me a joke. 'What's brown and sticky?' I didn't know. 'A stick!'

I know it was stupid but I fell about laughing. I should have rolled my eyes or groaned but I got the giggles. It was nice to laugh. Jake came over at one point. 'What's so funny? Your face is red.' I made Cayla retell the joke. He rolled his eyes AND groaned. 'Cayla, you've got a terrible sense of humour.' Then he smiled and went over to James and Owen.

'He's nice,' said Cayla. 'Yeah,' I said. 'The best.'

Friday 6th October
Two things happened today.

When I got in, Dad was helping Harvest stand up. 'Sit down, Leez. Someone wants to say hello.' As soon as I was on the sofa, he let go. She stood for a few seconds, looked up at me, then took a step! 'G'wan Harvest! You can do it! Walk to Leeza!' Dad was well excited. I waggled my legs and opened my arms while she teetered on the spot. She took a couple of steps forward. Fast and stumbly at first but she made it across the room before falling on my knees. We cheered and she giggled. I don't think she knew why.

The second thing is funnier. At tea time, Mum was going through Kenny's book bag. 'What's this?' she said. She was holding a teddy. 'That's Archibald,' he said. 'He's here for the weekend.'

Mum went pale. She rooted through his bag, searching for something else. 'Mac, there's a notebook. Not again. We've got the blinking class teddy! Why do teachers do this to us?'

Mum hates class teddies. This is the first time it's happened in Applemere but she says it's the same everywhere. She started to rant. 'I hate this pressure! Not only do we have to look like a normal family - impossible! - we have to fill that notebook with a bunch of photos showing all the fun we've had this weekend. We weren't going to HAVE any fun this weekend. I was going to clean the car and do the food shop. I bet any money that notebook's already filled with sickly-sweet photos of competitive parenting. What are we going to do? Plonk Archibald next to Harvest's dirty nappy bags? Put him next to the overflowing piles of laundry? What a disaster.'

By the time I'd left the table, Dad was rubbing Mum's back as she made a list of photos she could stage.

Saturday 7th October
Mum was right about the notebook. Last week Archibald went horse riding. The week before, he visited a paint-your-own-pottery gallery somewhere in Ambleside. The week before that, he was on the London Eye.

I can see why Mum wants to fake Archibald's weekend with us. It's not just kids who feel peer pressure.

Sunday 8th October
'Get your bikes, put on your helmets, and stand by that hedge,' was the first thing I heard as I got out of the shower.

It was supposed to look like a family bike ride. Archie (as we've come to know him) sat on the handlebars of Kenny's bike. Dad took the photo because he had the longest arms. As soon as it was taken, we took off our helmets, wheeled our bikes back across the road, and went into the house.

The second one was during Sunday dinner. Mum made a roast. It was exactly like Christmas Day. All the veg and potatoes were in the middle of the table. She lit candles, put a vase of fresh flowers in the centre, and combed our hair before we could sit down. Archie sat in the middle of the table with all the food around him. We couldn't start eating until Mum had taken a million pictures.

Afterwards, Mum went upstairs to print off the photos, and make up a paragraph about Archie's weekend with the McAuliffe family. It was a good job she missed it. As Spike grabbed the last two roasties, he knocked the gravy jug flying. It was like slow motion. The gravy splashed into the air in one long flow before landing slap bang over Archie's face. Spike looked properly scared. He stared in shock with his mouth open and looked at the door. The one Mum had just gone through. Luckily Dad was in charge. 'Let's sponge him down and hope for the best, eh?' was what he said.

We'll all be glad when Archie goes tomorrow.

Monday 9th October

When I came out of the loo at lunch time, Poppy was washing her hands. I'm not sure what came over me. I suddenly felt brave. Maybe because she was deliberately ignoring me, or maybe because Lexi wasn't with her. I knew I needed to say something. I didn't stop to think. I stood next to her at the sinks and took a deep breath. 'I get it,' I said. 'You like Jake so you're jealous of me. But it's not nice to be... not nice. Be nicer. You'd be happier.'

Yeah, it wasn't the best use of my vocabulary. It's not nice to be not nice? I walked out with my legs shaking and my cheeks glowing red. I'd sounded stupid but at least I'd had the last word. And next time I see her picking on someone, I can step in. She's no one to be scared of. In fact, she looked a bit pathetic as I walked away.

Meanwhile at home, Mum's much calmer. It's ridic how a cuddly toy could cause such a meltdown. I was just thinking about that in the loo. (It's where I have my best thoughts!) Even though it was a stupid class teddy, Mum acted just like Grandma. She felt she had to put on a show to fit in.

I promise you, Auction Bidders, I will never put on a show for a teddy bear.

Tuesday 10th October
Harvest's walking is getting well good. We still clap when we remember, but it'll have to stop at some point. Wouldn't it be great if people clapped whenever I walked down the road. It'd perk me right up.

Wednesday 11th October
Literally nothing happened.

Thursday 12th October
I'm definitely maturing. I can tell. When I was sorting my bag before bed, Mum came in. She said, 'We need a family meeting. Make sure you're here on Sunday, yeah?' I'm not sure where else she thinks I'll be. 'Sure,' I said.

The mature bit came next. I said something I've been thinking for ages. 'We don't have to have a meeting whenever you want to tell us something, you know. You could just tell us.' She looked up. I'd got her attention with my excellent point. Announcing she wants to tell us something in a few days seems like a waste of a few days. But she wasn't having it. 'Then no one would get a chance to say what they think. It's a democracy. We all get to voice our opinion.'

I've said it before and I'll say it again. This family is not a democracy. And if it were, I'd vote to ban family meetings. At least I didn't feel panicked this time. Whatever the announcement is, I'm sure it'll be fine. See? Maturity!

Friday 13<u>th</u> October
I'm still calm. The last couple of meetings proved it's not always bad news. It's time I remembered that. Besides, it's easy to feel calm when it's Family Fooday!

When I walked in from school, the whole house smelt of cooking. 'It's stew,' Dad said, as I stared through the oven door. A four-hour stew means we don't need to light the fire.'

Mum and Dad were working at the kitchen table and Harvest's chair was close to the oven. As close as possible without her being able to reach it.

Rich people have it easy when it's cold.

Saturday 14th October
I had the longest lie in which was good. I had the biggest amount of homework which was bad.

Sunday 15th October
We were ready (except for a sleeping Harvest) at 3pm around the table. I was calm. No sitting up straight, no steadying myself for terrible news. I looked relaxed. And inside, I almost felt it.

Mum jumped straight in. There was no build up. 'Me and your dad have been invited to Gina's 40th.' Gina is Mum's friend. I last saw her at Mum's 40th in Stockford. She was wearing a boob tube and Grandma's date chatted her up. (It's funny to remember Grandma before Will. The date she brought hadn't lasted long. I can't even remember his name.)

I'd started to daydream. Remembering parties we've had and people we don't see any more. When I switched back on, Mum said, 'So that's the plan. Something to look forward to, isn't it?'

I had no idea. What was happening and should I be looking forward to it? If I were typing this, I'd do a shrugging emoji.

Monday 16th October
I thought I'd have to ask Spike but I'm not sure he'd tell me the truth. As it turned out, I didn't need to.

'Are you excited about your weekend away?' Jake asked first thing. This was news. Were we all going to Gina's party? She lives in London and it'd be well expensive for a hotel. 'How do you know about that?' was what I actually said. He waved his phone at me. 'Mum and Molly message way too much. But hearing the McAuliffe news is better than hearing how your mum thinks I should ask you out.'

That was a shock. 'She never said that, did she?' Jake shrugged. 'Mum asked Molly if she'd be OK if I did and she said it'd be fine. So Mum told me I should ask you out because Molly was on board. Pathetic.'

Cait and Mum gossiping about us makes me MAD. At least Mum had the sense not to tell me. From what Jake says, it's a regular topic of conversation for him. At that point, the bus arrived, and I forgot what we'd been talking about. I only remembered half way to school.

'Where am I going for my weekend away?' was one of the odder questions I've asked him.

<u>Tuesday 17th October</u>
So I'm not going to London or Gina's 40th. That's just for Mum and Dad. Instead, as soon as I'm back from school on Friday, we're getting in the car, driving to Manchester, and staying at Grandma and Will's. It's not what I'd have chosen but it'll be a nice change.

<u>Wednesday 18th October</u>
Mum asked me for my fashion opinion this evening. I laughed in her face but took it as a compliment. She doesn't need me to tell her what to wear. But it was nice she pretended.

I lay on her bed while she went through the choices for Gina's party. The dress she wore for Grandma's wedding still fits. 'Miraculous!' she said, as she zipped it up. I thought it looked too posh but Mum reckons it'll be dressy. 'You should tell Jenna you're visiting,' Mum said. 'Arrange to see her on Saturday or Sunday. Grandma'll drive you round.'

That idea made me smile. Massively. I told Mum she looked good in everything she tried on.

Thursday 19th October
I messaged Jenna. She replied with, 'Yes McAuliffe! Get round mine. I'll remind you where you came from!' We're meeting up on Sunday and I can't wait.

When I came to bed, there was a line of bin bags on the landing. One for each of us. Mum and Dad, however, have packed themselves a suitcase. Typical.

Friday 20th October
Break up for half term.

I was buzzing all day. I don't know why. When we lived down the road, I was always at Grandma's. It was never exciting. But now? It's been ages and I had butterflies. (The good kind.)

The drive took forever. 'No idea why we thought leaving in rush hour was smart,' Mum said to herself as we crawled along the motorway. We got to Stockford at 8.25pm. Grandma took our binbags inside and Will dropped Mum and Dad at the station. They were getting the 21.15 train to London and were panicking they'd miss it.

Once they'd gone, I soon forgot about that. Grandma had been baking. We sat around the table eating chocolate cake and drinking juice. It wasn't a balanced tea but it was lovely.

Grandma's house has two spare rooms. Me and Harvest are in one of them and the boys are in the other. I've definitely got the better deal. Harvest's been asleep since 8, on a little mattress on the floor. I've got the whole of the bed to myself. In the other room, Kenny and Blane are top and tailing with Spike. Gross! I'd rather eat sweetcorn.

(You need to know how much I hate sweetcorn for that to make sense.)

<u>Saturday 21st October</u>
'Do you have homework, Leeza?' That's how Grandma woke me up. There are better things to hear first thing. 'No,' I said. 'It's the holidays. I'll do it in the week.'

When I was dressed I heard her next random question of the day. 'Who wants to help with the polishing?' As if! Luckily, Will stepped in. 'Excellent idea, Ursula, but it's me that wants help. I need someone to come to the park. I know it's a lot to ask. Especially when it'd mean breakfast in the café and playing all morning. Can anyone help?' Spike started cheering, so Blane and Kenny did too. Harvest looked confused. Next thing, we're all putting on our coats, and walking out of the house.

It was windy but brilliant. We rolled down the grassy hill, had a kick about with Spike's football, and went to the café for eggs on toast. It was the thickest toast ever! By the time we got back, we were all sleepy. I took Harvest for a nap but ended up dozing myself. Even though I live in the countryside, I was outside more here than I would be at home.

I miss parks. It was one of the things we used to do.

Sunday 22nd October
A day with Jenna is ALWAYS fun.

'Yalright, McAuliffe! D'ya recognise the place or are you looking for all the sheep?' she shouted as I got out of the car. We waved Will off and went inside. Nothing - literally nothing - had changed. I said, 'Hello Jenna's dad,' and waved. He was watching the match on the telly. 'Well, well, well, Leeza McAuliffe. You're taller!' Jenna pulled a face and dragged me upstairs. It was exactly like old times.

She asked about Jake. I found myself telling her about the kiss. ('Woah, McAuliffe, that's brill!') and that he was getting mithered by his Mum to go out with me. ('Why not? He's nice. You like him!') I didn't explain why not. It wasn't my info to share. But I made it clear it was never going to happen. 'We're best friends. Like brother and sister. It'd be like going out with Spike.' She made pretend sick noises and clutched her hands to her throat. That was all the explanation she needed.

By the time Will picked me up, we'd chatted our heads off. Even funnier was when I got back to Grandma's. Spike had a duster in his hand and a face like thunder.

Monday 23rd October

Mum and Dad got an early train back from London. They turned up at Grandma's in time for lunch. Will cooked mushroom, leek, and stilton pie, and Grandma made a crumble. We were fit to burst as we loaded our bin bags into the car.

Before we left Manchester, we did a detour. Dad said, 'While we're here, I thought it'd be nice to visit Grandma Jeanette again.' Within ten minutes we were pulling up outside the house. It still looked empty. Like no one loved being inside.

She answered the door, and made a shushing sound before smiling and patting everyone on the head. (Not Mum and Dad. Just us.) She whispered, 'He's just dropped off. It was a long night.' We ended up sitting outside the back door. Grandma Jeanette got a couple of garden chairs for Mum and Dad and she sat on the step with us. Harvest toddled around, and showed off her walking.

We weren't there long. GJ looked sad and it made me sad to be there. Except when Harvest walked, GJ gave a big smile and cheered with her arms in the air. So that was nice.

I've still not met Dad's dad.

Tuesday 24th October
My grandmothers are very different. Grandma Jeanette is sad and has a lot on her plate (Mum's words) whereas Grandma Ursula is off her head. (Also Mum's words.)

It's her birthday soon. A big one. Mum asked about it yesterday at lunch. 'What are you planning for your

70th, Ma?' She wanted to know if there was another party for the calendar. Apparently Gina's was 'an absolute blast' because 'it was nice not to be surrounded by kids'. Charming.

Grandma's answer disappointed her. 'Did I not tell you? Will booked a cruise. We'll be in the middle of the Caribbean for my birthday bumps.' Will laughed and squeezed Grandma's shoulders. He'd been carrying plates to the sink and was on his way back to the table. Mum rolled her eyes, Dad said, 'Nice,' and I thought it was a good idea.

Those were all the reactions I could see. It's not that interesting but it means I don't need to worry about party clothes again.

Wednesday 25th October
I made a deal with myself. If I started my homework this morning, I'd walk to Jake's this afternoon. I can't work all the time.

We were in his room. I told him about Grandma Jeanette and how I've still not met Dad's dad. 'Does it bother you?' he asked. I didn't know. I suppose that means it doesn't. If it did, it'd be clearer. I was lying on the bed with my legs up the wall. Jake was on his chair. On the other wall was the card I'd made him. The one with all the people in his life. I kept seeing Doris' photo looking at me. I should have made her head smaller. She's only someone from the village.

Then we got talking about Jake's dad again. He's been thinking about him a lot recently. That's what he said. And whenever he asks Cait, she shuts him down. 'She says he's not worth knowing and I'm better off without him. But what if I'm the same as him? What if I've got his personality? Because I'm nothing like Mum. What if I turn out to be not worth knowing too?'

I told him he was wrong. Of course he was worth knowing. And even if he were like his dad and not his mum, he was a good person. 'If you weren't, I wouldn't put up with you,' I said. He smiled, but not for real. That's when I thought of something actually useful to say.

'You might not be like Cait, but you know who you're like? Tom. Yeah, exactly like your grandad. He's kind and funny and helpful. He always makes sure everyone's OK. Whether that's his daughter and grandson, the new neighbours down the road, or the village when it's festival time. You're just like him. You're just as kind as he is.'

He snapped out of it then. 'Awwww, you soppy thing.' He smiled and gave me a hug. 'Ignore me. It's been on my mind. Since I started thinking about who I am, you know.'

'I know,' I said. And I meant it.

Thursday 26th October
Period.

Friday 27th October
Jake messaged. He said THX 4 CHAT. ONE DAY I'LL TELL MUM ABOUT THE GAY THING. NOT YET. I sent back NO WORRIES X

He messaged again a second later. THAT'S THE 1ST TIME I'VE WRITTEN THAT ABOUT MYSELF. I didn't know what to say so I sent a load of emojis. Mostly fist bumps, muscley arms, and smiling faces. He replied with a smiley face and that was that.

How strange to have to explain who you are to people who've known you forever. If I had to explain to Mum that I was left-handed, it'd be ridiculous. She'd say, 'I know you're left-handed. So what?' It's sad it's not always like that for people who want to date the same sex. Or for people who are born in the wrong body. Or for anyone who feels different from the way people think they are.

I like being left-handed. It's how I was born and it's part of me. Dad said that in the olden days, teachers forced left-handed children to write with their right hand. WHY??? How STUPID! Thank goodness people got over it and things changed.

Saturday 28th October
Heavy rain all day. It would've been a perfect Film and Duvet Day if I hadn't had loads of homework.

Mum brought up a glass of juice while I did my Geography. 'Will you get it all done tonight?' she asked. I shrugged. How did I know?

It is now tonight and I can confirm, I did NOT get it all done. Booooo. And with the clock going back an hour I had even more time than usual.

Sunday 29th October
Dad sent me for nappies before Tom shut the shop. When I got there, he was on a ladder stringing up Halloween decorations. I know it's a bit kiddy but I felt excited. The chilly weather, the darker evenings, the spookiness of it all... it's nearly my favourite time of year.

Mum won't let us say it. Not yet. She yelled at Spike when he tried the other day. 'We are NOT ready for THAT time of year,' she hissed. 'It's still summer.'

It really isn't. And here in my diary, I can say anything I like. CHRISTMAS, CHRISTMAS, CHRISTMAS CHRISTMAS, CHRISTMAS!

Monday 30th October
Back to school.

It was definitely darker when I got off the bus. Not like actual night time but not as light as before the holidays. It makes a real difference if you enjoy the season you're in.

Spike, on the other hand, was fed up. We'd used the last of his carrots for tea. Blane said, 'We could bury the scraps so more will grow.' I thought that was cute but Spike looked exasperated. (Great word!) I saw him sitting with Blane after tea, explaining the process of carrot growing. Neither of them looked like they were enjoying the conversation.

Tuesday 31st October
Halloween!

Miss Wilkinson gave out a page of spooky Maths problems. For fun. (Not my kind of fun but she tried.) Eg, A witch is shopping for a broomstick in the sale. It's 10% off every broomstick. If the original price is £19.99, how much does it cost now?

I guess she had the Maths problems already. Like it was an old worksheet but she added in some spooky things. Still, it made school feel more lighthearted than usual.

I told Jake about it on the bus. He was mad. 'We never got anything like that,' he said. 'I miss Miss Wilkinson.' That made me think it was just for the babies. Class 1 is still the youngest even if I'm in the older half.

I thought about that later when we were playing duck apple. Spike's head was soaking and then Kenny went face-first into the bucket. We burst out laughing but he started to cry. Then he started to laugh as Dad towelled him off in a silly way.

Am I too grown up for this? I thought to myself as I looked around at the mess we'd made. Water everywhere, half eaten apples, and everyone soaking wet. Probably, I decided. But that doesn't mean I'm not having a good time. A brilliant time, tbh.

11

The Worst Of Times

<u>Wednesday 1st November</u>

As soon as I walked in, Mum was waiting with the craft box. 'Quick as you can, Grandma needs a birthday card. I want them posted by five.' It was 4.04pm.

I don't know why Mum left it so late. Or why she couldn't send one from Moonpig. Instead I had the most stressful half hour of my life. It's hard to be creative when you've got someone pacing up and down, saying, 'For the love of God, Leeza, I thought Kenny was slow. Will you get a flipping move on!'

Dad said he sprinted to the postbox like Linford Christie (who?) and made it in the nick of time. Five cards are now winging their way to Grandma, who'll have already left for her cruise when they arrive. I didn't say that to Mum. There was no point.

Thursday 2nd November
Tom and Billy were in the village as we got off the bus. They were sorting wood for Bonfire Night. People have been leaving old crates and garden waste outside the pub to be moved on the back field. 'Give us a hand, lad,' Tom shouted to Jake as we walked past. 'No chance,' Jake muttered under his breath, but shouted, 'I can't. Me and Leeza have a project!'

We went to Jake's room. There was no project but we caught up on each other's gossip. I had very little.

Friday 3rd November
Grandma flew to her cruise this afternoon. She had to meet the boat in the Dominican Republic. We looked on the map. Then we tracked her flight on an app. It left on time. That's all I can tell you.

I don't think I'd like a birthday on a boat. I don't mind boats any other time, but for my special day, I'd want dry land. I'm glad I've worked that out before it's an issue.

Saturday 4th November
Grandma is 70!

After a few tries, we managed a FaceTime. 'How's the birthday girl?' Dad asked, as soon as she came on the screen. 'Tiddly!' was her reply. They'd just finished lunch (it was nearly bedtime here) and we could see a bottle of champagne on the table. 'Seventy is the new thirty-five, Molly. That means I'm younger than you!' Mum said, 'Course you are, Ma. We'll have to go clubbing.' I could tell it was her sarcastic voice. The one she uses when she says things like, 'Sure you can stay up late on a school night, Spike.' Or 'Thanks so much, Harvest for puking over my top.'

We know Mum's sarcastic voice well.

Sunday 5th November
It must be strange being seventy. It's really old. But then sometimes it's not. On the FaceTime, Grandma was wearing a vest top and sarong. That's what Mum

would wear. (It's what I would wear, if I had a sarong.) She was also using FaceTime. Some old people can't do that. Plus, she was laughing her head off. Other old people sit in their chair and look sad. She definitely wasn't that.

It's like Tom. I think he's a similar age. But all weekend he was lugging planks and boxes onto the field for tonight's bonfire. Like a young person could. And Auction Bidders, it was worth it.

I met Jake outside the pub and we walked to the field. The fire was massive. Tom had started it straight after closing the shop. It'd been going for ages when we turned up. I got as close as I could and felt my cheeks glow red. It was lovely. I asked Jake about Tom's age. He's seventy-two. 'He did well to sort the fire,' I said. 'Nah, he loves it.' Jake replied. 'Gives him something to do.'

Later, when we'd watched the fireworks and the fire was calming down, Cait came over. 'Nice to see you love birds having fun,' she said. She walked past before we could say anything. (And what I'd want to say would get me in trouble.) It makes no difference. She won't be told.

Monday 6th November
Before the bus had even pulled away, Jake said, 'Sorry about Mum last night.'

It's not as bad for me. I think it's funny she's got the situation upside down. Jake, on the other hand, is fed up. 'She thinks she's being clever but she's not. Even if we WERE seeing each other, it'd be annoying how often she goes on about it.' He gave a big groan and looked out of the window. I felt sorry for him. Cait thinks she knows a secret - that he's seeing me. He isn't, but he's still got stuff he's keeping to himself. It would be bad if he's forced to tell her before he's ready, just to shut her up.

I told him that. Except it only came to me in second lesson. (Science. I'd drifted off after hearing the word 'friction'. It made me think of Cait and Jake.) He agreed he should take his time. 'I know she'll be fine. She won't care if I date boys, girls, or anyone. She's not bothered about any of that. She just needs to stop winding me up.' I nodded. There wasn't much else I could do. Then Jake said something that made me feel sad.

'The person I'm worried about telling, is Grandad.'

Tuesday 7th November
Tom is the kindest, friendliest grown-up ever. He was like a surrogate grandad before we had Will. The idea that he'd be mean to Jake if he knew he was gay, is awful. He couldn't possibly be.

Except maybe he could? Maybe he's never met anyone who's gay before. Maybe he's lived in a small village all his life. Maybe he's friendly to everyone who lives there but not to outsiders. No, that can't be right. He welcomed us and we were from miles away. But maybe if Mum was married to a woman, or Dad was married to a man, he mightn't have been so nice.

I really hope I'm wrong and that Tom is kind to Jake. Jake thinks the world of him. It'd be awful if that changed.

Now I'm worrying about Jake all over again.

Wednesday 8th November
After stressing about Tom all night, Ms. Phelps has told us to read 'Goodnight Mister Tom'. It's our class book to go with our World War 2 learning. I started it at lunch time. The Tom in the book is much grumpier.

It's mad to think that Grandma is as old as the war. The first part shows how children from the cities were evacuated from their families and sent to the countryside. I can't imagine that. Well, I can imagine leaving a city and moving to the countryside. Obvs. I've done that myself. But leaving my family behind would be hard.

Also, I've just checked on my calculator. Grandma is NOT as old as the war. She'd kill me if she knew I'd written that.

Thursday 9th November
We're supposed to read up to Chapter 5 for Monday but I've just finished Chapter 10. I always read on. How can I stop when the story hooks me in? Besides,

I was right. 'Book Tom' is nothing like 'Village Tom'. 'Village Tom' is always smiling. He'd take in loads of evacuees if they needed him. He'd make sure everyone felt safe.

Yes, Auction Bidders, I get what I'm doing. Bigging up Tom so I forget how hurtful it'd be if he pushes Jake away. 'Book Tom' might do that but not 'Village Tom'. That's what I'm telling myself.

Friday 10th November
Grandads are like buses. You wait ages for one and then three come along at the same time.

(That's the sort of joke Dad makes, whenever we have a run of something. And the three I'm talking about are Will, Dad's dad, and Tom. If you hadn't worked it out.)

Saturday 11th November
Homework: Boooo. Reading: Yay.

Sunday 12th November
Bored, bored, bored.

Monday 13th November

Because my book's about the olden days, I went back through my History book to Grandma's interview. It took ages to transcribe so it's only right I gave it another look. Here's a bit about her favourite Christmas present.

> GRANDMA: I was six years old when my mother finally convinced my father she needed a vacuum cleaner. I don't think he'd realised how hard it was to keep everything clean. She had to scrub floors and beat the rugs out of the back door. But that's what women did. They wanted to keep a clean home. When the vacuum arrived, it was wonderful. It picked up fluff, and crumbs, and dirt in no time. She would run it up and down, over the carpet, and it'd be good as new. Even Father had to admit it was worth every penny. I don't think he'd ever seen Mother so happy. I'd follow her around the room in my socks and stare at the stripes it made in the tufts. Up and down I'd go, following in its wake. Then one Christmas morning, there was a present at the end of my bed. It was wrapped in paper. As high as a bike but not as long. I didn't have a clue. But when I opened it, I was thrilled. A toy vacuum cleaner! I couldn't believe my eyes. From that day on, whenever Mother cleaned the floors, I'd follow behind with my very own cleaner. I felt like such a grown-up lady.

Tuesday 14th November

Grandma's interview explains a lot of things. If she watched her mum scrub floors and beat rugs, no wonder she loves her Henry Hoover and sprays polish every five minutes. Those things are easy in comparison.

But why did her mum not tell her dad to get off his bum and do his share? I can't imagine living in a home where Mum does all the cleaning and Dad 'lets' her have a vacuum cleaner. She'd tell him to get lost in seconds.

There are times when the world feels unfair. There are other times when I can see I'm lucky I was born when I was. Just think how easy people in 50 years will have it. Except for climate change. That's bigger than all of us.

Wednesday 15th November

I was telling Jake about Grandma's cleaning. He thought it was funny. He also couldn't imagine Cait doing all the housework. In Jake's flat, there's a rota on the fridge. Everything gets split three ways. Jake moans but I think it's nice. It'd feel like I was equal with the grown-ups.

Thinking later, I changed my mind. I'd hate to clean the toilet after Spike's used it. Maybe it's good that in my house, the really grim chores are split between Mum and Dad.

Breaking news! Jake's just sent me an email. HERE'S SOME OF TOM'S INTERVIEW ABOUT HIS CHILDHOOD. MAKES YOU THINK. I've just printed off the attachment. 'Makes you think' is right.

```
All the wages in the village came from the farms. Animals were
sold for meat, crops and vegetables were harvested and sold, and
then there was the dairy side of things. From the age of, ooh I
don't know, about ten I s'pose, I was milking cows for pocket
money. Some months they'd be overrun with farmhands, other times
they'd need anyone they could get. That was good news for a local
lad that wanted to earn a few bob. I remember driving a tractor
for the first time. As long as your legs reached the pedals, no
one minded. I'd be about thirteen, there or thereabouts. No talk
of health and safety back then, mind. Work needed doing, and
that's all anyone cared about. I do remember how tiring it was.
No chance of a sleepless night. Not after a day in the fields.
As soon as my head hit the pillow, I'd be spark out. Best way,
I reckon. What did I need with school and lessons? I learnt
everything useful out and about, working hard and making ends
meet. The supermarket's a doddle after that. What a time! I
remember it like it were yesterday.
```

I don't know why but after I read that, I felt churned up. I was in the same village, 50ish years later, and that life had gone. The new estate, the row of shops, even my own back garden, were all on land that used to be farmed. It made me wonder how much change I'll see as I get old. Not as much as that, I hope.

Thursday 16th November
I've had another think. It'll be OK to see changes for the better but not the worse. I want Jake to feel comfy with his family. That would be a good kind of change.

Friday 17th November
There was frost on the path, first thing. Lunchtime was freezing and I forgot my gloves. It was nice to get home and feel the warm of the fire.

Mum and Dad still haven't cracked it. You'd think Friday Fooday would be a casserole, or a roast, or a pan of chilli? Think again! It was homemade baba ghanoush, veggie sticks, and potato salad.

Summer food in front of a fire should only happen when you're camping. Not mid-November, sitting in your kitchen, having shivered all day.

Saturday 18<u>th</u> November
Mum spent the day sorting wardrobes and digging out our jumpers. She must have realised baba ghanoush wouldn't keep us warm.

Dad took Blane and Spike out on their bikes. Blane wasn't keen but he went anyway. That meant the house was quiet for a few hours. Apart from when Harvest ran into the living room wall. There were lots of tears and she has a little mark on her forehead but she's fine. I stayed out of the way.

Can you tell today was boring? Maybe not for Harvest, Blane, and Spike, but defo me.

Sunday 19<u>th</u> November
I finished 'Goodnight Mister Tom'. I really liked it. In the end, Tom wasn't as grumpy as he first seemed. And it made me think of Will, 'Village Tom', and Dad's dad.

It's strange that my actual relative from that list, is the one I've never met.

Monday 20th November
I woke up to a message from Jake. He'd sent it while I was still asleep. OMG. MUM'S DOING MY HEAD IN. I CAN'T EVEN.

By the time we met at the bus stop, he'd calmed down. 'What happened this time?' I asked. 'Same as usual,' he said. He sighed as he shook his head. Then the bus came and he had to act normal in front of everyone.

Is it good to put on a brave face? Not every day, just sometimes? When there are people around who don't know something's up, is that a help? Is it good to be distracted? Or should I encourage Jake to talk about his feelings? It's hard to know what's best. Maybe ranting on a message is enough. It seemed so this morning.

School was boring. Nothing's happening atm. Maybe it's me that needs the distraction. The last thing Jake said as we got off the bus was, 'Another night of listening to Mum say how brilliant you are.' I smiled and said, 'Sorry.' He smiled back. 'Not your fault.'

In another universe, he'd be a lovely boyfriend to have. In this one, I just want him to be happy.

Tuesday 21<u>st</u> November

Grandma and Will flew back from their cruise. Dad propped the iPad up on the table while we ate tea. 'What's Ursula's flight number?' he shouted to Mum. She was changing Harvest in the living room. 'No idea,' she said. Eventually he picked up her phone to see what Grandma had said, and then logged into the flight tracker app. We stared at the screen the whole time we were eating. Just as the plates were being cleared, the plane took off. Dad cheered. The rest of us had forgotten what we were waiting for.

Two things.

1. Mum and Dad look at each other's phones all the time. When they need info like flight numbers or what date something's happening. But if they did that to my phone, I'd go mad. I hope they know to keep out of my business.

2. Tracking a plane is boring. Sorry but it's true.

Wednesday 22nd November
Three weeks on a boat is ages. I don't think it's for me. Mum said, 'There were 15 messages from Ma when I woke up. Basically, she's landed.' Dad kept buttering his toast and said, 'Any news?' 'No,' was all Mum said.

Fifteen messages saying nothing is hard to do. Even for Grandma. There's not much news from anyone these days.

Thursday 23rd November
Me and my big mouth. There's been news today. Oh yes there has.

Tomorrow, straight after school, we're driving to Manchester. All of us. At first I thought we were seeing Grandma and Will. They'll defo have presents for us, but no. Mum said, 'Your dad's had a call from Grandma Jeanette. Seems like his dad is close to the end.'

What a strange way of saying it. 'Close to the end.' Like he's near the top of an escalator or coming out of a tunnel. Or the end of a roller coaster ride or holding the end of the toilet roll. Sorry. It seems weird to be silly but that's what I thought when she said it.

Dad's quiet but OK. Mum said he knew it was coming so it's not a shock. She's just been in. She sat at the end of the bed and said, 'I thought you'd want to know what's going on.' I did, but she's never said that before. Progress! Then she said, 'Do you have any questions?'

I couldn't think, so I said no. But now she's gone, I've got loads. Where will we stay in Manchester? Will we see Dad's dad? What will he look like? And how's Grandma Jeanette? I don't feel sad. Is that bad? I feel sorry for Dad but he didn't get on with his parents for years. If Grandma Jeanette hadn't got in touch, everything would have carried on as normal. It's a strange one. I should feel something but I don't.

Friday 24th November
I'm writing this in the car. (My school bag's blocking anyone from seeing.) It's been pouring all day and it's rush hour on the M6. Fun. (Not fun.)

Spike's moaning about being squashed, Blane's crying to himself because he's worried there might be thunder, and Harvest's pooed in her nappy. We can all smell it. Kenny has done the only sensible thing and fallen asleep. I'm writing this because there's nothing else to do.

Mum says we'll get to Grandma's in a couple of hours. We're staying there tonight. If it's not too late, Dad will visit his dad. We might go tomorrow. There's nothing else to say. The traffic is slow. Mum's phone has just rung and she's answered it. Blane is still whimpering. Spike's still grumbling. Mum's just told him to pack it in...

Something's happened. Mum's face when she turned round, looked awful. She's gone white. I don't know who's on the phone. All I can hear is her side of the conversation. 'Where is he now?... What have they said?... Was he breathing?'

It must be Grandma Jeanette. But why has she rung Mum and not Dad. I don't know who else it'd be. It sounds like the conversation's nearly over. 'Don't worry about a thing. We're on our way.'

Yeah. Defo Grandma Jeanette. Mum's talking to Dad in the front but I can't hear properly. Dad looks white too. But he already knows his dad is 'near the end'. Why is it a shock now? And why are we coming off at this junction? We're nowhere near Manchester.

Oh God. I feel sick. Mum's just told us.

The call was from Cait. Tom's had a heart attack.

<u>Saturday 25th November</u>
We got home at eight. It was still raining. Mum went to the mini supermarket to get Jake because Cait had gone with Tom in the ambulance. Jake's going to stay with us until Cait can come back.

He'd been crying. I could tell. I wanted to hug him but I didn't. Not with everyone watching. I told Mum we should put the airbed in my room, like when Jenna stayed. She looked at me for a moment before saying, 'OK. If you want.'

Even if me and Jake were boyfriend and girlfriend, the night his grandad has a heart attack would not be the time for kissing on a mattress. Even she could see that.

He told me what happened when we were lying in our beds. 'It was so fast,' he started. 'I'd been back from school for a bit. I was still wearing my uniform. I came down to get a Coke. He was behind the till. He looked a bit weird. Like when he feels rough after a night on the beers.' He paused for a second, took a breath, then carried on. 'I asked if he was OK and he said, 'Course I am, lad.' But he looked worse. And he was rubbing his chest. Then he groaned. It was a horrible sound. I thought I'd heard all his sounds but not this one. Then he fell back and slumped down against the shelf.'

Jake looked at the fairy lights as he talked. The ones he'd helped put up. Like he couldn't look at my face while he shared everything. I thought it'd be better for him to keep talking. I waited a moment before saying, 'And then what happened?' He swallowed a couple of times and sniffed. 'I shouted for Mum. She was upstairs. Then I got my phone and called for an ambulance. I was doing that when she came down. She screamed when she saw him. The woman on the phone kept talking at me, I can't remember what she said. Lots of questions. I remember telling her that my mum was a nurse. And Mum was getting Grandad flat on the floor and undoing his top button, checking him over. And she was shouting at me to help. I ended up kneeling next to him. The whole time he had his eyes closed and was making groaning sounds.'

He stopped. I knew the rest from Mum. Tom was rushed to hospital. He had an emergency operation and is in Intensive Care. Cait's been with him the whole time. The doctors say it's too soon to know.

Sunday 26th November

Dad finally made it to Manchester. He went after breakfast. I overheard him talking to Mum as he repacked his bag. 'It feels wrong to leave now. I don't think I can do this.' Mum said, 'Yes you can. You need to go.' Then they hugged for ages.

I didn't mean to spy. I was at the top of the stairs, waiting for the bathroom. But I felt sorry for Dad. There's a lot of bad news atm. My stomach's in knots.

Last I heard, his dad was comfortable.

Monday 27th November
Period.

Jake's still here. He's getting good at putting on a brave face. He can relax with me but when he's watching Peppa Pig with Harvest and Kenny, he pretends he's having fun.

We've talked loads. Mum says I've to keep the bedroom door open when we're in there. I've not argued but she should have said the same when Jenna stayed. We could have been girlfriends for all she knew. Because Jake's a boy, it's different. That's not fair.

Her suspicions have upsides though. Last night me and Jake were sitting up, talking in our beds, and the door barged open. No knock or anything. Mum had two mugs in her hands. 'Hot chocolate?' she said. Really casual, like that happens all the time. As soon as she'd gone, I rolled my eyes. 'Not subtle, Molly Hart-

McAullife,' I said. Just to me and Jake. I didn't let her hear me, obvs.

It wasn't like she'd interrupted a serious conversation. We'd moved on from that. Ten minutes earlier, Jake was saying how he needed Tom to get better. 'He can't die before he knows the real me. That would suck so much.' His eyes had glistened and he'd cleared his throat. Then my throat started to feel massive and my eyes prickled too. I got out of bed and squeezed his shoulders.

Mum turned up when I was back under my covers and discussing the best cheese. (Me: Halloumi, Jake: Babybel.) It was definitely a better time to interrupt. And even if it was an excuse to snoop, hot chocolate in bed was brilliant. Thanks Mum!

Cait's been ringing every evening. I feel sick when I hear the phone. Still no news.

Tuesday 28th November
I know I moan about school sometimes (OK, all the time) but it's been good to have to stick to a normal

routine. Even if me and Jake are arriving at the bus stop and walking back home together, the day feels less stomachy. School has turned into a decent distraction.

Wednesday 29th November

It was during last lesson. There was a knock on the door and a boy from Class 3 handed Ms. Phelps a note. She read it, then said, 'Leeza McAuliffe? Miss Wilkinson wants to see you. In the office.'

My stomach lurched. No one's ever sent for me before. My head started to buzz. I got up from the desk - my legs were like jelly - and walked to the door. I heard whispering. 'What've you done? You in trouble?' Oscar, I think. Before I closed the door, Cayla gave me a supportive smile.

The office is near the main reception and gets used for meetings. When I got to the desk, I told Miss that I'd been sent for. 'Ah yes,' she said. 'Go straight in.' I couldn't tell from her voice. Was I about to be told off? Or was it bad news? The sick feeling raged as I opened the door.

The first thing I saw was Jake. He was sitting opposite Miss Wilkinson. He looked up as I walked in. His eyes were red and there was a box of tissues on the desk in front of him. That's when Miss spoke. 'Leeza, thanks for coming so quickly. Jake wanted you to hear the news. Do you want to tell her or shall I?' I was about to burst with stress so I snapped. 'Just tell me. What's happened? It's Tom, isn't it?'

Jake looked at me. Then smiled. Then he started to cry. Then smiled again. 'He's going to be OK. Mum rang school. He's awake, they've done tests, and he's going to be OK.'

My smile filled the room. I laughed out loud even though there was a lump in my throat. Then I walked round the table, wrapped my arms around Jake's neck, and squeezed tight. Neither of us could speak properly and we couldn't stop cry-giggling. Miss Wilkinson let us stay in the office for the rest of last lesson. There was no way we could go back to class. We were too giddy. As I sat there, I felt the weight of the past week float off into the distance. Tom was going to be OK. That was AMAZING.

Thursday 30th November

Last night was loads of fun. We've had a sleepover every night but it's loads better when there's nothing to worry about. I even joked with Mum. 'As it's Jake's last night, I think we need hot chocolate. Just so you've got an excuse to snoop again.' She didn't even blink. 'I don't need an excuse to snoop on my own children but I'll bring you hot chocolate because I'm as happy about Tom as you are.' She smiled as she said it so I hope she's joking. (About the snooping.)

Jake dropped his clothes off in the flat first thing. I waited at the bus stop. Cait had got back from the hospital in the night so he saw her too. When he came back outside, his eyes were red. She's annoyed him this year but it must've been hard without her for a week. 'You OK?' I said. He nodded and sniffed but couldn't say anything without his eyes filling up. He needed a distraction because the bus was about to come. 'Look at this video. It'll take your mind off things.'

I handed him my phone. For the whole journey, Jake watched a video of Spike and Harvest singing 'I'm a

Little Teapot'. On repeat. Every so often he'd look at me with a face that said, 'Why do you even have this?' but he kept watching. When the bus pulled up to the school gate, he was back together. He handed me my phone. 'Ta Leez. I'll never unsee that.' Then he put his arm around my shoulders and we walked into the building together. When Poppy saw us, she was livid. Good.

I'm writing this in bed and thinking about everything that's happened. It was nice to have so many chats with Jake. I'd say we're closer than ever but it's also nice to have my privacy. I'm looking at the airbed and remembering everything we talked about. Now I can hear Mum coming upstairs. I think she's gone to check on Harvest. Because I'm alone in my room again, I can hear every little sound. Harvest's door has just closed. Now Mum's footsteps are coming towards my room...

Oh.

Dad's been on the phone. Grandad Dougie died a couple of hours ago.

12

Happy Families

<u>Friday 1st December</u>

I told Jake at lunchtime. He already knew but let me tell him anyway. I said, 'I should feel sad but there's nothing there.' He said, 'You don't have to feel anything. There's no right or wrong with things like this.' I'm not sure I agree but I'm glad he wasn't judging me.

When we got off the bus, Billy and Dave were dragging cables out of the back of the pub. 'Christmas lights!' Billy shouted, and pointed up at the pole. 'Making things nice for Tom!' We watched as both men unrolled a load of cable before moving their ladders into position. I didn't stay long. I love Christmas lights but I was cold and wanted my tea. They'll be there tomorrow.

Saturday 2nd December

Dad's still in Manchester. He FaceTimed last night and seemed OK. He even made a joke about Grandma. When Mum asked how he was, he said, 'I'm going to drown in tea. Ursh is forever brewing up.' In the background we could hear Grandma shout, 'I heard that, Sebastian. No cake for you with those insults!' Their usual banter made things feel better.

More news came at lunch time. Mum got a message to say Tom would be coming home in the next few days. She read it out and we all cheered. Even Harvest. She was in her highchair eating yoghurt with her hands. When she clapped, it splattered everywhere.

Mum suggested we give the Wooltons some space. 'Tom'll need his rest, and Cait and Jake will want family time with him.' She's probably right but I miss Jake. Also, the Christmas lights aren't on yet.

Sunday 3rd December

It was just before tea when we saw headlights on the drive. Dad was back! Mum told us to get to the front door so we could shout WELCOME HOME. By the time we were in the hall, his key was already in the lock. I'm not sure coming back is so great. Not after being at Grandma's with all her cake.

He gave us a big smile and hugged everyone, especially Mum. Then they kissed. YUCK.

Monday 4th December
Grandma Jeanette's friend is staying with her. Kathy someone. Dad remembers her from when he was a teenager. He said, 'If Kathy's anything like she was, that funeral will be planned with military precision.'

Jake asked me if I was OK. He keeps doing that. I tell him I'm fine and then he moves on. The thing is, I AM fine. But I feel guilty about some things.
- That I don't care enough about Grandad Dougie, who is my actual relative.
- That I'm actually angry with Grandad Dougie for refusing to see us for years. How DARE he.
- That I feel loads more for Tom, who I only met last year.

I didn't say any of that to Jake. We're both pleased Tom's on the mend and coming home. No one needs to hear my feelings about it.

Tuesday 5th December

It's that weird time of year when the days are full of festive activities alongside end of term assessments. Today we had a Maths test. I don't think it went well.

When I got in, Mum asked about it. I said, 'I didn't understand some of the questions, let alone know the answers.' She thought for a moment and said, 'That's your teacher's fault. You weren't born with Maths in your head. Someone has to help you put it there.'

I can't say that to Miss Wilkinson. Can you imagine? 'I failed the test because you didn't teach me properly!' Ha. I'd love that. No, I'll be keeping those thoughts to myself. But just by Mum saying that, I stopped obsessing over it. Sometimes sharing a worry gets rid of it.

The afternoon was much better. We practised Christmas carols. It was lovely! We're doing a concert at the old folks home again. Singing is defo better than multiplying.

Jake's been busy this week. He's doing shifts in the shop to help out. As soon as he was off the bus, he was through the doors and behind the till. I waved through the window as I walked past. I hope he's OK.

The Christmas lights still aren't on.

Wednesday 6<u>th</u> December
It was the English test today. I found it easier but I'd still rather not. Carol practice in the afternoon made things better.

When we got off the bus, Dad was up a ladder outside the supermarket. 'I've been roped in!' he shouted. The lights are now up but they don't work. 'Not yet but soon,' was what Billy said when we asked. 'That grandad of yours makes it look simple,' he said to Jake.

It's great everyone's helping but I really want the lights to be on now. December's nearly over. I need festive cheer.

Thursday 7th December

And now I feel guilty again! How can I have festive cheer when Grandad Dougie's funeral's still to come? It's on Monday. That's all I know. Mum said she'd tell us more when they'd decided what to do.

Jake was behind the till again after school. I went with him this time. Mum had texted me. WE NEED A BAG OF BROWN RICE AND ANY STIRFRY VEGGIES YOU CAN FIND.

When I walked in, I was too busy searching for rice to see what was going on. But then I looked up. Tom was there! 'Ohhh!' was all I could say before I rushed over.

I didn't try to hug him but I jumped up and down instead. It was SO good to see him. 'Too nippy outside so I'm having a walk past the tinned fruit.' Jake was shaking his head behind the till but he was happy. We all were. Considering Tom's just out of hospital, he looked amazing. Before I left, he picked up a box of posh biscuits and handed them to me. 'For putting up with my lad.' He nodded his head towards Jake. 'Thank you, Leeza. I've already spoken to your mum and dad, but they told me it was all you.'

I felt like crying. It was lovely of Tom to say that but it wasn't just me. Everyone 'put up' with Jake. I thought about keeping the biscuits for myself. He hadn't told me to share. But when I got in, I put them on the table with the rice and veg.

I made sure everyone knew I was being generous though.

Friday 8th December
I know more about Grandad Dougie's funeral.

Dad told us during Family Fooday. He said, 'We want to let you know what the plan is. See what you think.' This sounded suspiciously like a family meeting on the wrong day. I guess Sunday's a bit late when the funeral is on Monday.

Dad said, 'It's happening at the crematorium at 11am. I'm going and if you want to come with me, you can. If you don't, that's fine. You can stay with Grandma.' He looked around at us. 'Does anyone have any questions?'

I've realised that when people ask me that, I need time to think. Questions never come to me straight away. This wasn't the case for Spike. He had loads. 'Will we see his body? What's a crema-thingy? Will everyone be in black? What happens when it's finished? Do we have to go to church? Will there be food?'

'Great questions, mate. Let's do them one at a time.' By now my pasta bake was getting cold, so I ate while I listened. Dad said, 'You won't see his body. It'll be inside the coffin at the front. You'd be sitting on a bench, like when school takes you to church. You don't need to wear black, although it's nice to look smart and sensible. The crematorium is where the service takes place. Sometimes there's readings and songs. It depends what's been arranged. At the end, the coffin goes one way and the people go out the other. And yes, there'll be food. There's a buffet in the pub.'

I was still eating. None of those were questions I'd had, but now I knew the answers I felt comfier about going. Not that Grandad Dougie deserved us being there. Why should he? He was never there for us. But that's a bad thing to say and makes me feel guilty to even think it. So, I'm going. Deep down, Dad wants us there, anyway.

There was only one thing I was wondering. 'Is Grandma Jeanette very sad?' Dad paused for a moment and looked at Mum before answering. 'I think she probably is,' he said. 'But she's strong. And living with my dad wasn't easy. When I left on Sunday, Kathy was there with a bottle of wine and they were about to watch 'Bridesmaids'. She's keeping her spirits up.'

Kathy sounded like a good friend. If Jake's ever upset again, we'll watch films with a bottle of pop.

<u>Saturday 9th December</u>
We've all decided to go to the funeral. Except Harvest. She's going to stay with Grandma. Lucky for her, she's too young to be given chores.

Mum asked me what I wanted to wear. I had no idea. Nothing in my wardrobe looks funeral-y. In the end, we settled on black leggings, my black boots, and my navy-blue jumper dress. It's warm and is a darkish colour. Mum said no one will care that there's a big robin on the front.

She had a harder time with Spike. The only smart trousers he's got are his school ones. 'There's no way I'm having a day off school and still wearing my uniform,' he said. He had a point.

Sunday 10th December

We got to Grandma's for lunch. The house smelt amazing. Will was basting the roast potatoes when we walked in. 'That smells good, Ma,' Mum said. Grandma snorted. 'That'll be the joint of beef. Don't worry, there's a nut roast thingamajig for you and your brood.' Mum ignored her and helped us hang our coats.

The 'nut roast thingamajig' was lovely. And we still got potatoes, veg, stuffing and gravy. After we'd finished,

Dad left to see his mum. She said everything's organised but he wanted to check.

I'm writing this in Grandma's spare room. Harvest's travel cot is next to me. She's woken up four times since I've been in here. Looks like I won't be getting a good night's sleep.

I wonder if Grandad Dougie is in heaven. I wonder if there IS a heaven. I wonder if he ever wondered about me. I hope tomorrow isn't too sad.

Monday 11th December
What a long day! I dozed off in the car on the way home. Mum said there was a point around Lancaster when we were all asleep. (Except her and Dad.)

The funeral was better than I thought. OK, it was strange at first. We walked into the crem just before 11 and there was a bunch of other adults waiting there. Dad said some of them were friends and some were neighbours from the street. Grandma Jeanette was sitting next to Kathy in the front row. She gave Dad a hug and patted Mum's arm. We sat behind them.

Everything was quiet. Then some slow music played as six men walked in carrying the coffin. Mum called them undertakers. I kept thinking how that sounded like 'underknickers,' which was silly. My head kept making me think of funny things.

Once the coffin was put down at the front, a woman started speaking. She said we were very welcome and that we'd gathered today to say goodbye to Douglas. I'd never heard him called that before. Although when you think about it, I didn't know he existed before May. Dad looked serious. His eyes pointed down to the floor. I could only see the back of Grandma Jeanette but she sat very still.

At one point the woman made a sort of joke. She said, 'I'm sure you all know that Dougie didn't suffer fools gladly.' Some people laughed politely but Grandma Jeanette turned to Kathy and said, 'She's not wrong about that!' Everyone heard, they laughed properly, and things felt relaxed. For a few seconds at least.

There was more music, more talking, and then it was over. The coffin went behind a curtain and everyone walked outside. It was sunny. That's strange for December.

The pub part was more fun. People chatted and the buffet was nice. Grandma Jeanette sat at a table with us and thanked us for coming. She said, 'Molly, you've done wonders with this lot. I'd hate to lose touch once everything settles.' For the first time that day, she looked like she was about to cry. 'Course you'll see us,' Mum said. 'Look, we haven't worked out what we're doing yet, but you're more than welcome for Christmas.' I saw Dad's face. He was standing behind her seat when she said it. This had definitely not been discussed. But then he rubbed Mum's shoulder and said, 'Absolutely. There's loads of space.'

I looked at Mum. She was doing that thing she tells us to do. She was being the bigger person. Years ago, Jeanette and Dougie (probably just Dougie when you think about it) pushed Dad away because they didn't like Mum. And now she was being the bigger person and inviting her for Christmas. I'm not sure I could do that. I'd never invite Poppy, that's for sure.

By the time we left for home, we'd been hugged by lots of old people, picked up Harvest and our bags from Grandma's, and set off in rush hour traffic. (We always time our motorway journeys badly.) When we got back to Applemere, we went straight to the chippy.

The funeral was better than I expected, but the chippy tea was the highlight, no question.

Tuesday 12th December
I woke up at 08.34. That's the exact time the bus arrives! Argggh.

Except NOT argggh! As I ran out of the bedroom I bumped into Mum. 'We're having a duvet day,' she said. 'The McAuliffe family needs nice things.' What a legend she is! (Sometimes.) We dragged our duvets down to the living room while she brought us toast on the sofa. 'Right gang,' she said. 'We've an important decision to make. Which Christmas film shall we watch first?'

By the time it was dark, we'd boxed off 'Elf', 'Home Alone', and 'Muppet Christmas Carol'. After a rubbish couple of weeks, it's beginning to look a lot like Christmas!

That's a song, btw.

<u>Wednesday 13th December</u>
After yesterday's relaxing film fest, things feel normal again. Noise, bustle, and panic. The McAuliffe chaos is back.

It's Mum's fault. She was on her laptop looking at the calendar. 'There's only 12 days 'til Christmas and I've done nothing. No food, no presents, no decorations. I want to go to sleep and wake up in January.' Dad was changing Harvest's nappy or he'd have said something useful. Instead it was left to me. I went with, 'That's bad. What are you going to do?'

I was trying to sympathise but it sounded like I was having a go. 'I'll think of something,' she said. But then she put her head in her hands and breathed deeply. I came to bed early to get out of the way.

Jake's just messaged. THE MUMS AV BEEN GABBING ALL NIGHT. GOD KNOWS WHAT ABOUT. GLAD UR BACK. THE BUS IS NO FUN WHEN UR OFF.

Even though there'll be no Christmas this year, it's nice that Jake missed me.

Thursday 14th December
The Christmas lights are finally on! Better late than never. Apparently Tom had to sit on a deckchair outside the shop, shouting instructions to Billy up the ladder. I'm just happy they're done. So far there's been too much non-Christmas stuff happening.

Friday 15th December
Jake gave me a clue this morning. 'Have you heard? They're hatching a plan.' He was talking about The Mums. I hadn't heard a plan but they tell me nothing. 'Are you going to fill me in?' I asked. He shrugged. 'They're working out the deets today. I guess we'll find out later.' That was infuriating. (Excellent word!) All he knew was Mum and Cait were plotting.

I found out later. It was announced during Friday Fooday. Mum said, 'We've been having a think.' That could mean anything. 'It's been a rough few weeks. First Tom, then Grandad Dougie, then your Dad being away, and me trying to work and look after you lot... Christmas has taken a back seat.'

I knew this but Spike looked shocked. 'You're not cancelling Christmas! No way, Jose!' Dad shushed him and Mum carried on. 'I was talking to Cait and she's had it tough too. With Tom slowly getting better, covering the shop shifts, and all the worry at the hospital, they've not had a chance to get organised either.' Mum was smiling so it couldn't be bad news. I tried to relax. 'So me and Cait have had a brain wave. It's great when you think about it.' I sighed and waited for the bombshell. 'We've decided that... we're all going to Cait's for Christmas!'

Whaaaa? I had questions but I let her carry on. 'We'll replace Christmas dinner with a Christmas buffet. You'll choose one present and we'll order them for January - give Father Christmas a break, yeah?' She aimed that at Harvest, who didn't care either way. She went on. 'It'll make New Year more cheerful and make life easier over the next fortnight. It'll still be a lovely Christmas day. But with Tom, Cait, and Jake. We'll play games and eat food but it'll be a group effort. Like having more helpers to make it work last minute.'

What about Grandma Jeanette? Is she coming too?' I said. Had everyone forgotten she'd been invited? 'Good point, Leez,' Dad said. 'I had a chat with her yesterday. She rang to thank us for the invitation but she's going to stay in Manchester for Christmas. Kathy's cooking and they're going to make cocktails.' He chuckled as he shook his head. It sounded like she was OK. 'We'll have her visit in the New Year.'

This might just work. It'll be cool to spend Christmas with Jake. And Mum and Dad are more relaxed when Tom's around. Maybe Christmas isn't ruined after all.

Saturday 16th December

Jake was round first thing. He said he needed space from home. In no time, we were talking about Christmas.

'I think it'll be good,' he said. 'The same as usual but with more of us.' 'But no presents,' I said. 'Or roast potatoes.' That had been Spike's first question. 'What about the roasties?' He'd said it as soon as Mum had finished talking.

'I've been roped in to making a cheese cake.' He rolled his eyes. 'I made Mum a birthday cake last year so she's decided I'm the next Jamie Oliver.' He laughed. 'I'll have to make two with all the McAuliffes coming.'

It was fun to discuss even if the plans are different. Christmas Day without roasties will be weird. But mixing things up and looking forward to a January present will good. Jake seemed quiet. I hope he's not disappointed we'll be there.

Sunday 17<u>th</u> December
Mum has made a lot of lists for someone planning a calmer, stress-free Christmas.

Monday 18<u>th</u> December
Only 4 more days of school. Woohoo.

Between the funeral, the Tom-stress, and the talk of a smaller Christmas, I'd started to worry I'd never feel the glow. You know, the one I get this time of year? Luckily it's been growing all day.

Carol practice was lovely. We sound good and we'll be ready to visit the old folks on Wednesday. Then there were the village lights. Obvs I know they're there but I still shiver when the bus turns into the high street and I see them for the first time.

Jake was quiet again. Even though school's fun and there's no proper work, he still seems worried. I hope he's OK.

Tuesday 19th December

'Just call me Gordon Ramsay!' Jake said, as he came out to the bus stop. 'Do I have to?' I said. He was smiling. For real. Something had gone on.

'Last night I made a practice winter berry cheesecake with raspberry coulis and it was AMAZING. I'm going to rock your world on Christmas day!' He sounded happier. Relaxed. The bus arrived as he was showing me the photo. It looked impressive. 'Some other stuff's happened too but I'll fill you in later. Meet at lunch?'

We sat on the bench. It was freezing. Everyone else was inside - eating slowly so they didn't have to be out in the cold. We had loads of privacy.

He started to speak. 'I wanted to catch you up on what's happened.' It sounded serious but a big smile filled his face. 'What is it?' I said, 'You can't stop grinning!' It couldn't be bad news but he was taking far too long.

'Last night I'd made the cake and was drizzling the sauce when Mum came into the kitchen. She said, 'You'll make Leeza a lovely husband if you can cook like that.' 'Oh,' I said. 'Exactly,' he replied. 'It made me mad. Even if we WERE dating, it's a stupid thing to say. I'm 14! She needs to get a grip. I tried to ignore it like normal but I couldn't. Then she said, 'Take a piece into school. She'll be really impressed,' and I just snapped. I told her I wouldn't be giving you any cake because you weren't my girlfriend. And even if I liked girls, that wouldn't mean I'd go out with the daughter of her best mate. And it's a good job I prefer boys to girls because she doesn't know anyone with a son my age, so she can't go on about it all the time like she's got a glitch in her system.'

'Wow,' I said. 'Yeah,' he replied. 'I hadn't meant to blurt it out but I couldn't help it.' She was quiet for like, three seconds. Then she pulled me towards her and squeezed me far too tight, and said, 'That's great news.' Then she cut us some cake.

My face beamed. 'That's brilliant,' I said. 'You've told her and she's supportive. Now she'll back off talking about us all the time. 'Yeah,' he said. 'But as she was getting the plates, I looked up and saw Grandad in the doorway. He'd heard everything.'

My stomach lurched. All my butterflies flew in at the same time. This was exactly what Jake had worried about. 'Oh no. What did he say?'

Jake took a breath then did a perfect impression of Tom. 'He said, 'Fair enough, lad. I always thought your mum were barking up the wrong tree. C'mere,' and he gave me a big wrestle-y hug. Well as much as he could with his scar still healing. Then he messed up my hair.'

I laughed. I could picture Tom doing exactly that. 'After that, I pretended I needed the toilet so I could have a cry. A happy one. I've never felt so relieved.' I put my head on his shoulder. I was happy for him. He said, 'I'd never have found the courage if I hadn't talked to you first. Thank you.'

I'd done absolutely nothing. But it was nice to hear.

Wednesday 20th December

The choir visited 3 old folks' homes. Everyone thought we were great. (Well, the old people that stayed awake, did.) It was nice to see the decorations as we sang. We haven't put anything up this year because of 'everything' but when I got home, Spike was wrapping tinsel around a bush in the garden.

I don't care about the tree. It's the lights I'm missing. We're taking our decs down to Cait's at the weekend. Mum says it's to create a combined Christmas atmosphere. It's a lovely idea but they haven't seen

Spike's yule log he made in Nursery. (An empty loo roll, painted brown, with a green blob for holly. It's out every year and I'm always disgusted.)

Thursday 21st December

More carolling and more old folks. Today's homes were livelier. Maybe because we visited in the morning? I get tired after lunch too.

The best bit, obvs, is breaking up from school. Christmas might be different this year but finishing school always feels amazing.

Mum's just popped in. 'Have a think what present you want. I'll be ordering soon.' I nodded. I don't really care. A new diary, I suppose, but that's not very big. Not that I expect big things. Maybe some clothes? Remember how much thought I put into what I wore to James' party? A new outfit for parties would be good. Hopefully there'll be more of those in the future.

Friday 22nd December

I woke up to Christmas music playing. 'The McAuliffe-Hart Consultancy Agency has closed for Christmas!'

Dad said. He was still in his PJs even though it had gone 10am. (That's normal for me, not for him.)

He was feeding Harvest while Mum was kneading dough. 'Whose bright idea was this?' she muttered to herself. Apparently, 'making bread' was on her list. Surely if the Christmas buffet is supposed to be easier, she should have just bought a loaf? I didn't tell her that. It wouldn't have gone down well.

The best bit about everyone being busy is we had a cheese board for tea. My favourite!

Saturday 23rd December
Apparently, it's All Hands On Deck Day. Like that's a real thing.

I had a quick shower then the next thing you know, I've got my arms full of decorations, walking down to Jake's. Dad, Blane, and Kenny came too. Spike stayed and helped Mum in the kitchen. They're desperate to channel his energy into cookery. I'm just not sure I want to eat what he makes.

Tom let us in. He's got to do gentle exercise every day. That means he's on door duty. 'These two think they've been given a lazy license,' he said, pointing to Cait and Jake on the sofa. 'Not now the decs have arrived!' Cait said. 'Take a seat Dad, this is a job for us.'

We all helped. Tom stayed seated but told us whether things were straight or not. Blane was in charge of crawling behind the furniture to plug things in. I put decorations on the tree as far as I could reach and Jake did the high parts. Cait stood on the arm of the sofa and tied bunting to the curtain rail.

When you see posh people's houses in magazines, their decorations match. There's a theme or a colour scheme. One year, Grandma did everything in cream and gold. When you look around Jake's flat, there's also a theme. It's a mis-matched mess! It'll never be in a magazine and Grandma would have a fit. But you know what? When I stood back and looked at our handywork, it looked great.

Except for the toilet roll yule log. I hid that round the back of the tree.

Sunday 24th December

Mum's list has been stuck to the fridge for a week. It's tatty, got loads of scribbles, and you can't read what's left to do. I think she's regretting giving Spike food responsibilities. This morning he was knocking on the toilet door saying, 'Mum, my cheese straws are ready.' Her voice said, 'One minute!' but I could guess what her face was doing.

The best bit (apart from it being Christmas Eve) was that Grandma and Will surprised us. Dad saw their car from the window and said, 'Mol? Are we expecting your mother?'

We were not. It didn't matter. It meant Mum was forced to have a break (she needed one) and it meant Dad had help with Harvest and Kenny. Will had only been here 5 minutes before Kenny was climbing all over him and Harvest was hugging his legs. 'We've come to see if we can salvage your Christmas!' is what Grandma said. She was trying to wind Mum up but she didn't rise to it. She just looked at her and said, 'Lolz.' Proper sarcastic.

With them here for a couple of hours, it was like normal. The iPad played Christmas tunes, Dad handed round a box of mince pies, and Grandma had brought presents.

She took her time. There was lots of chat while she pretended there was no massive bag by her feet. Eventually she couldn't pad it out any longer. 'I suppose it's time for some gifts. Who will be Santa's little helper?' Straight away, Spike's, Blane's, Kenny's, and Dad's hands shot up. (Dad was joking.) I didn't join in. I'm twelve.

Blane handed me my gift bag. Inside was a new diary (yay!) a posh pen (nice!) and a set of books. They're fiction but set in different historical periods. I'm going to start with the one about the girl in World War Two. Thank you, Grandma!

Happy is such a nice feeling to have. Sometimes life gets in the way and it isn't there. When I feel happy I have to spot it and enjoy it. How lovely to feel happy at Christmas. I'm so lucky.

Monday 25th December
Happy Christmas, Auction Bidders!

What with Mum's lists and Dad's jobs, this week's been crazy. But so far, today's been really chilled. I've just come up to get dressed. We've all been in PJs and dressing gowns since we got out of bed. And even though Mum told us we'd get a present after Christmas, she still surprised us.

When I woke up there was a pillow case at the end of my bed. I pulled it towards me and could feel some little things at the bottom. Can you believe it? I actually said, 'No way!' to myself.

Inside was my favourite fruit (a pear) my favourite crisps (Skips) and my favourite treats (marzipan fruits). There was also a party popper, a pencil sharpener, and a bouncy ball. 'Don't make me regret the party poppers!' was what Mum shouted across the landing.

By the time we'd come downstairs some people (Spike) had no favourites left because they'd eaten them in bed. Dad made a big pile of toast and put the plate on the living room floor. The Christmas tunes played, Harvest danced to herself (well, she stood on the spot and bent her knees in time to the music) and Mum and Dad drank a whole pot of tea.

We had a nice call with Grandma Jeanette on speakerphone. She sounded much happier than the last time I saw her. (Obvs. It was a funeral.) She chatted to us while Kathy clanged pans in the kitchen. 'She thinks she's Nigella,' she said. It was nice to hear her make a joke.

Now I'm dressed and Mum's shouting at me to get my coat. Dad's loaded up the food in the wheelbarrow. I've just looked out of the window and there're more wine bottles than food tubs. I'm leaving now. Off to have a combined, simpler Christmas with Jake and his family. I can't wait.

Tuesday 26th December
We got back at 2am!

Even though we weren't at home and even though there was no Christmas dinner, yesterday was just right. Also, to keep Spike happy, Cait had made a bowl of roast potatoes to go with the buffet. (Thank you, Cait!)

It was a tight squeeze in the flat but we managed. I was cross-legged on the floor most of the time. The hardest part was playing Twister. There was no room to fall over! The food was really nice. Even Spike's efforts. Tom kept saying, 'You've kept this to yourself, lad,' as he ate one of the cheese straws. 'We'll have to get you on a Harvest Festival stall. Doris on the cakes, you on the pies.' Spike beamed his head off.

Tom's allowed a small red wine now and then, and he has to eat sensibly. Mum's all over healthy eating so that was fine. He also has to move regularly. At one point, so he could have a stretch, he took Kenny and Blane down to the shop for a lemon. (For Cait's gin.) As soon as he'd gone, Mum said, 'How is he?' Cait said, 'Really good, considering. We've been so lucky.'

Luck is like happiness - a nice thing to have. You just have to be grateful when it's there.

After we'd eaten and Dad had done the washing up, there was a tinkling noise from the chair. Tom was tapping his glass with a spoon, trying to get everyone's attention. 'SHHHHHHH,' Spike hissed. (Like it had anything to do with him.) Tom got to his feet. 'Time for a speech, I think.' Cait said, 'Oh no, he's off,' and Jake put his hands on his face like something terrible was about to happen. Everyone laughed.

'While you're all here I wanted to say how much a part of our family you've become.' He was looking at Mum and Dad but then smiled at the rest of us. 'When I had my little episode, you went above and beyond to keep Jake out of trouble. And Cait said how marvellous you were. I'm just sorry to have caused all that bother.' 'Nonsense!' shouted Dad. Mum agreed. 'Give over, will ya.' Tom waved his hands towards them like they were talking rubbish (I should try that!) and carried on. 'It just goes to show that family is where you find it. You're very much a part of our family and that makes me happy. To the McAuliffes!' Tom raised his glass. Everyone shouted, 'To the McAuliffes,' which felt mad because that's us. Then Mum jumped in with, 'To the Wooltons!' and everyone repeated it after her.

It was at that moment I stopped feeling guilty about Grandad Dougie. Like, COMPLETELY. He'd chosen not to know us. What an idiot! It wasn't my fault. It was his, and he'd missed out. Because actually when you think about it, we're all pretty great.

The food was out all day. It was impossible to stop picking. In the end I moved to the window which was the furthest place from the table. The sky was getting dark but it'd become a strange purple colour. 'Mind it'll try and snow tonight.' Tom had joined me. 'That'll be a turn up.' I smiled. I don't think we'll get that lucky. Besides, there's been enough luck already. Tom stayed where he was, looking at the sky. Then he said, 'I heard you've been a good friend to that lad of mine. When he didn't think he had anyone else, he could turn to you. Thanks lass. You're a good'un.'

It's silly but my eyes felt stingy. I blinked a few times and smiled. Later, when Cait said, 'So it looks like you're not going to be my daughter-in-law any time soon,' I was prepared. I said, 'You couldn't handle it, Cait.' She burst out laughing and high-fived me.

<u>Wednesday 27th December</u>
I had an epic lie in.

<u>Thursday 28th December</u>
We FaceTimed Grandma and Will for their 1st wedding anniversary. Grandma said, 'We're just having a romantic breakfast in bed.' Mum pulled a face and said, 'Then you shouldn't have answered your phone.' She's right. If I'd been rung before I'd got out of bed, I'd be fuming.

We hadn't woken her. On the bedside table was a coffee pot with a plunger, a toast rack with one slice left, and two empty eggshells in the egg cups. 'I know how to treat a lady,' Will said. They were propped up by pillows with their legs under the covers and newspapers on top. 'What are you doing tonight?' Mum asked. 'We're not sure yet. An expensive, romantic restaurant, maybe?' 'Right,' Mum said. 'Sorry I asked.'

Later Dad said it'd be a bag of chips in the bus stop. We all laughed.

Friday 29th December
This diary is practically finished now. I've been flicking through. I never did find out if I have any talents. I'm a whole year further on in my life, and I still don't know if I'm good at anything. It made my insides ache when I realised that.

Jake spent the afternoon here. Cait had taken Tom for a check-up and he was bored on his own. I showed him my diary. Not the inside, obvs, but the fact it's nearly full. 'I started this year trying to work out who I was and what I was good at,' I said. He looked at me. 'Why?'

I flicked back to January to get it exactly right. 'Grandma got highlights because she said 'New Year, New You,' and I thought that was cool. But I didn't know who the old me was and I didn't want a new me until I'd found the old one. I've spent the whole year wondering what I'm good at and what makes me ME.' I felt the ache again. This time it was fiercer. 'I still don't know what it is.' He looked at me for a second. 'Does it matter?' he said. I blinked a few times and felt immediately annoyed. 'It matters to me,' I said. Then I stopped talking.

Saturday 30th December
It must have been playing on my mind because I've just snapped at Mum. Kenny had finished his dinner, including every bit of mixed veg. She said, 'Well done, Kenny. Aren't you good at clearing your plate.' I heard that and saw red. 'What about ME? What am I good at? I'VE been clearing my plate for YEARS.' I was about to storm off but Mum got up. She carried the dishes to the sink and said, 'You're good at everything, Leeza. Everything you put your mind to.' I gave it another ten seconds and THEN I stormed off.

Miss Wilkinson would laugh her head off if she'd heard what Mum said.

Sunday 31st December
We're leaving for the pub in 10 minutes. The Wooltons will be there and so will the rest of the village. I usually love a get together but I'm not feeling

it right now. Mum got a notification on her phone. My new clothes (my present!) have been dispatched. That cheered me up a bit. (I chose leggings, a black t-shirt dress, and chunky black boots. Mum asked if I was entering my goth phase. Lol)

Jake came round earlier. He brought back our food tubs from Christmas. (Kenny's building a tower with them as I'm writing this.) I didn't hear the door so I'd no idea Jake was here until I came downstairs for a drink. When I walked into the kitchen, him and Mum were deep in conversation. When they saw me, they both stopped. 'Oh... there you are,' Mum said. Like I'd be anywhere else.

It's nearly 7pm and I'm trying to finish this before we leave. I've been here ever since Jake went. I wasn't in the mood to be around people. I gave my room a quick tidy (I MUST feel bad!) and put my new books on the shelf. I can hear everyone else downstairs. It's noisy, as usual. Except someone's just walked up. Kenny, I think. (He must have finished his tower.) I can tell by the way it takes him longer to get up each stair.

OK this is weird. He's just pushed this note under my door.

> Leeza,
>
> Jake told us you don't know what your talents are, and Mum noticed you were wondering the same thing yesterday. It's easy with some people. They're brilliant at sports, or they sing well, or they get top marks in every test. When your gifts and skills are less specific, they're harder to see. But they're still there.
>
> Jake told us what a good friend you've been. He said you were the only person he could talk to when he felt scared and lonely. What a talent that is! And every school holiday, you spend your time keeping the little ones busy so we can work. That's incredibly helpful for our family. Cait and Tom always tell us how well-mannered you are. They're so happy you're Jake's friend. All the time Cait was teasing you both, she was just relieved you were so nice.
>
> If it helps, we'll make you a special badge that says, 'Leeza McAuliffe is the best friend, daughter, and sister in the world'. But we think you'd prefer that we don't. So have this letter that we've signed. Without you, this family would fall apart. Stick it in your diary, so whenever you doubt yourself, you can look back and remember what we think. You don't need to change anything. Keep being you.

They'd all signed it on the back. Sort of. Mum, Dad, Blane, and Kenny had written their names. Spike had too, but with the words 'they made me sine this' underneath. Harvest had done a scribble.

New Year, New Me? After reading that, I'm not sure I should change a thing. What a way to end the year! Even with all the stupid mushiness, it was brill to read. Maybe this family isn't as annoying as I think. Maybe it's nice to be part of a big gang. Maybe I like living in the madness.

Mum's just shouted up. 'Leeza McAuliffe, if you're not ready to leave in one minute, I'm cancelling New Year.'

On second thoughts…

Acknowledgements

For what feels like forever, the process of book-writing is solitary. You spend more time with the fictional characters in your head than the human beings in your life. At several points along the way, you question your sanity, screaming with frustration more than once. But then suddenly, other people arrive! Without them, the story would remain stuck. They are essential to the process, there'd be no book with their input, and this is where I thank them.

From the first draft, my writing group has been actively involved. Listening to extracts, pointing out issues, and pushing me to be better every fortnight. Thank you to Alex, David, Jan, Jane, Nigel, Sarah, Simon, Suzanne, and Vanessa. (But especial thanks to the hardcore regulars. They know who they are. Their fortnightly feedback has been invaluable.)

Huge thanks goes to Claire Dyer from Fresh Eyes. Her insights and support mean everything. I usually reach out for her editorial eye just when I'm tearing my hair out in despair. Her calm and encouraging feedback – as well as her clear critique of what's working and what's not – always gets me back on track. I couldn't do it without her.

Gary McGillivray from Portal Design and Illustration continues to interpret my incoherent blather to create a truly gorgeous book cover. Along with every other technical detail he deals with so capably, he makes the *look* of the book stand out and demand attention. And this time, there're illustrations! Thank you, Gary.

Many thanks to my family members who read through early drafts and told me what they thought. I'm forever grateful for their time and honesty. Thank you to Mary Bond, Frank Bond, Dom Bond, Monica Bartley Bond, Steve Rew, and Ashley Preston.

It's also been hugely useful to get a more youthful perspective on the story. Apologies to my family from the previous paragraph, but it's been a while since they were at school. That's why I'm so pleased to have had the input of Emily Kernick, Madeleine Dooley, Eva Blinston, and Tom Smith. They reassured this Xennial woman, enormously.

A special mention must also go to Matthew Blanchard. I knew it was important to get Jake's story right and Matthew's input was a massive help. I'm so grateful for his time, critique, and reassurance.

Finally, thanks to YOU. Yes, thank you to the readers who've found their way to Leeza and her antics. Being an indie author means relying on word of mouth. The marketing side can feel like a real slog after spending so long on the actual words. However you found this story, thanks for reading it. Knowing it's out in the world feels amazing and I'm really grateful you're part of that journey.

Nicky Bond was a Teacher and Learning Mentor before publishing her first book in 2017.

She lives in Merseyside, where she's a keen Liverpool FC Women supporter. She loves cooking, drinking tea, and has a small obsession with the Eurovision song contest. Her blog drops every Monday, and she spends the rest of her time as @bondiela on Insta and Threads.

LEEZA MCAULIFFE HAS LOADS MORE TO SAY

Milton Keynes UK
Ingram Content Group UK Ltd.
UKHW020910140524
442690UK00015B/552

9 780995 657458